Dear Reader,

When I was asked if I would rework a fairy tale for a Harlequin Presents series, I knew immediately which one I wanted to do. Admittedly when I was a child, my mother would read Tolkien and Douglas Adams rather than the Brothers Grimm, but I've *always* loved the tale of Red Riding Hood. The imagery is so striking—dark forests, red flowing capes, glowing yellow eyes peering out from the shadows. Staying on the path, veering off it, temptation, danger, empowerment... All of these things are deliciously irresistible to a writer!

Whether it was the traditional tale of the little girl outwitting the wolf with the help of the huntsman and saving her grandmother in the process, retellings like Angela Carter's or the film and TV adaptations, I was always drawn to the wolf. Was he bad or misunderstood? Was he the villain, or could he possibly be the hero?

And that's what I wanted to explore in *Taming the Big Bad Billionaire*. I hope you enjoy reading it as much as I did writing it.

Happy reading!

Pippa xx

Once Upon a Temptation

Will they live passionately ever after?

Once upon a time, in a land far, far away, there was a billionaire—or eight! Each billionaire had riches beyond your wildest imagination. Still, they were each missing something: love. But the path to true love is never easy...even if you're one of the world's richest men!

Inspired by fairy tales like *Beauty and the Beast* and *Little Red Riding Hood*, the Once Upon a Temptation collection will take you on a passion-filled journey of ultimate escapism.

Fall in love with...

Cinderella's Royal Secret by Lynne Graham

Beauty and Her One-Night Baby by Dani Collins

Shy Queen in the Royal Spotlight
by Natalie Anderson

Claimed in the Italian's Castle by Caitlin Crews

Expecting His Billion-Dollar Scandal
by Cathy Williams

Taming the Big Bad Billionaire by Pippa Roscoe

The Flaw in His Marriage Plan by Tara Pammi

His Innocent's Passionate Awakening
by Melanie Milburne

Pippa Roscoe

TAMING THE BIG BAD BILLIONAIRE

Recycling programs for this product may not exist in your area.

ISBN-13: 978-1-335-14862-9

Taming the Big Bad Billionaire

This edition published by arrangement with Harlequin Books S.A.

For questions and comments about the quality of this book, please contact us at CustomerService@Harlequin.com.

Harlequin Enterprises ULC
22 Adelaide St. West, 40th Floor
Toronto, Ontario M5H 4E3, Canada
www.Harlequin.com

Printed in U.S.A.

Pippa Roscoe lives in Norfolk near her family and makes daily promises to herself that *this* is the day she'll leave the computer to take a long walk in the countryside. She can't remember a time when she wasn't dreaming about handsome heroes and innocent heroines. Totally her mother's fault, of course—she gave Pippa her first romance to read at the age of seven! She is inconceivably happy that she gets to share those daydreams with you all. Follow her on Twitter, @pipparoscoe.

Books by Pippa Roscoe

Harlequin Presents

Conquering His Virgin Queen
Virgin Princess's Marriage Debt
Demanding His Billion-Dollar Heir

The Winners' Circle

A Ring to Take His Revenge
Claimed for the Greek's Child
Reclaimed by the Powerful Sheikh

Visit the Author Profile page
at Harlequin.com for more titles.

For anyone who ever got goose bumps
when they heard, "Are you sitting comfortably?
Then I shall begin."

CHAPTER ONE

'Always stay on the path,' her grandmother had said. 'For bad things lurk in the woods...dark things, monsters and wolves.'

But Little Red Riding Hood didn't listen to her grandmother because she didn't believe in fairy tales. Deep down, she knew that the most dangerous stories were the ones we told ourselves.

The Truth About Little Red Riding Hood
—Roz Fayrer

IT WAS THE smell of coffee, as strong and bitter as his quest for vengeance, that usually heralded the beginning of Roman Black's day, not damp earth and tree bark. It was the richly carpeted floors of his office that he usually stalked at this hour of the morning, not the crunch of twigs and leaves.

The noise felt overly loud, as if the attempt to be stealthy had made him clumsy. But if there was one thing Roman Black was not, it was clumsy. Every thought, every move, every action had always held one purpose for Roman, and one purpose only. And finally, after years, the end goal was now within his grasp.

Ahead of him Dorcas, the dog he had acquired for the express purpose of his visit here to the Occitaine region of France, loped with huge, graceful strides, occasionally stopping to cast a curious glance at its new owner, or to ferret out some invisible treasure at the base of a large tree.

Twelve hours ago, Roman had received the vital information that revealed his quarry had left a party on the outskirts of Moscow and returned to France to visit an ailing relative. Nine hours ago, he had arrived in France himself and took up residence in a small villa barely three miles from here. Seven hours ago he'd been interviewing for a canine companion at the local dog shelter—for what was more predatory than a single man alone in the woods? Let alone a man of Roman's imposing stature.

No. He had planned for this. He had worked out every possible variable. He needed to look, at the very least, non-threatening. Admittedly, he had thought to find something small and fluffy, perfect to lull his prey into a false sense of security. But Dorcas had been sitting there in the grey concrete cubicle, watching, as if she had known from the very beginning that he would come to get her. And whilst an Irish wolfhound was neither small nor fluffy, one look at her and Roman had not been able to stand the thought of such a glorious creature trapped in a cage. If he had been a more self-aware man, if, perhaps, he had had anything on his mind other than vengeance, he might have understood his decision better.

But as Roman stalked through the trees on his first reconnaissance of the woods where he knew he would find his prey—maybe tomorrow or the day after—he allowed himself to imagine the moment that victory would be his. That finally, after almost twenty years, he would make the old bastard pay for what he had done.

It was a sweet feeling, almost euphoric, rushing through his mind. Sublime in the sense that everything he'd ever wanted was nearly his, yet could easily be taken away at any moment. And it was while he was lost in that delicious imagining that Roman first laid eyes on his prey.

He stopped short. His breath stolen from his lungs.

For there she was, walking through the forest at this ungodly hour of the morning as if she'd just stepped out of the pages of his mother's favourite fairy tale. His eyes snagged on the black ball gown visible through the opening of a scarlet velvet cloak. The hood had fallen back to reveal the creamy swan-like curve of her neck, framed by tendrils of blonde hair that had escaped a complicated plaited knot. She was exquisitely beautiful. He'd known that, of course, from the photographs and extensive research he'd had his people compile. But nothing had prepared him for the effect of seeing her in person.

His swift gaze crossed her features back and forth, hunting for a blemish or flaw, but none were detectable beneath the overall impression of perfection. His pulse thrummed as he took in high cheekbones that perfectly framed an oval-shaped face, high arched brows that gave as much space as possible to large cornflower-blue eyes. Desire wound through him, as unwelcome as it was fierce, and he cursed this unexpected weakness within himself. The delicate arms holding the cloak against her waist looked almost vulnerable and for a moment he debated whether to stop, to turn back. But he knew he wouldn't.

She looked impossibly innocent—no sign of the hard edges that he had been forced to develop by her age of twenty-two years. How that had been achieved under the guidance of such a monster as Vladimir Kolikov he simply couldn't fathom, and as such cast it aside as an impossibility. Her beauty, her apparent innocence, was simply fancy dressing around one thing and one thing only.

The key to his revenge.

Exhaustion had settled deep into her bones and Ella barely knew where her feet were stepping. But years of summers spent walking the forest that bordered her grandmother's cottage had left the path indelibly inked on her mind and body. Her grandmother.

Ella's heart ached, worry and grief twisting in her chest like a living thing. She had been at a party in Moscow when she'd received the phone call informing her that her grandmother had been found unconscious at the bottom of the stairs in her cottage and taken to hospital. Ella's mind had gone instantly blank and if it hadn't been for her guardian she didn't know what she would have done. He'd arranged for a car to retrieve her from the birthday party of the British Ambassador to Russia, a private jet to fly her to an airfield just outside of Limoux, and another car to take her to the hospital.

If any of the hospital staff had thought it odd that she had arrived dressed in a ball gown and velvet cloak, none had said as such. The doctor had explained that her grandmother had suffered a broken hip and fractured shoulder from the fall but the knock to her head had been what had worried him the most. Strange medical terminology, stretching her usually quite good hold on the French language, had made her want to shake the man and demand he tell her that her grandmother was going to be okay. But after nearly thirteen hours in the hospital, Claudette hadn't yet regained consciousness and the medical staff had ushered Ella out of the building to get some rest. And to change. Because if she'd looked dishevelled when she'd first arrived, Lord knew what she looked like now.

When she'd asked the taxi to stop on the other side

of the woods, she'd given no thought to her clothing. Instead she'd wanted to make her way to her grandmother's cottage on the path that felt achingly familiar and yet strange and unknowable at this time in the morning. But the hems of the cloak and dress had dragged along the floor, soaking up the damp earth, making them impossibly heavy. As the material caught on twigs and thorns, Ella felt as if she were battling something physical, not just emotional, on her journey back to her grandmother's.

She pulled up short, wanting to wrench the damn thing from her shoulders, wanting to wail and shout and cry all at once. She forced herself to breathe in a long, slow breath, in and out. She had almost recovered when she heard the snap of a twig. The hairs on the skin of her arms rose in the early morning air, sending tingles and shivers down her back. Casting a glance around her, Ella's gaze snagged on something in the dense foliage and she took half a step towards the bush before she saw the gleam of yellow eyes staring at her. Before she could run, the beast crashed out of the tree cover and loped towards her in an alarmingly lazy gait that covered the distance between them in seconds and, just as it was about to pounce, she closed her eyes and—

'Dorcas, sit!'

Prising her eyes open, she watched as the massive beast careened to a halt barely a foot from Ella and sat on its hind legs, tongue lolling out of its mouth and a look of almost indescribable happiness at having found something for its master spread across its wolfish features.

An almost hysterical laugh of relief bubbled in her chest, until it caught there the moment she saw the beast's owner making his way towards her.

He was over six feet fall, more lean and lithe than broad, his every step almost graceful as he wove his way through the trees. Ella's heart thudded in her chest the moment he locked eyes with her, trapping her gaze as easily as the breath in her lungs. Longish dark hair swept carelessly around his head and hung down towards a low brow that appeared almost forbidding. Assessing eyes, squinting slightly against the pale morning sun, were a shocking shade of light blue, almost yellow, as if he shared some kinship with the animal which sat at her feet. Lips that were neither thick nor too thin made her wonder whether they would feel as perfect as they appeared to her... The fanciful thought momentarily startled her before she hungrily ate up what else she could see of him. The sharp edges of his cheekbones and jawline were strong and proud, and Ella's eyes tripped down to where the collar of his grey linen shirt peeked above a deep rich blue pullover, revealing a glimpse of the hollow that she inexplicably wanted to press her thumb to.

Ella's heart pounded in her chest. Never had a man had such an effect on her before. And never had her mind betrayed her with the errant thought that rang through her entire being.

This man is going to break my heart.

The shock and sheer ridiculousness of the thought made her shake her head, causing the figure to stop in his tracks. Ella used the brief respite to breathe. Despite his imposing stature, she couldn't sense any form of threat coming from him.

'I'm sorry about Dorcas—she gets excited when we meet other people.'

At this, the beast—*Dorcas*—decided its master's command had been lifted and she unfolded her giant frame and came close enough to nudge Ella's hand with her nose. As Ella absentmindedly stroked the huge hound, it took a moment for her tired mind to understand the source of her confusion because, although she understood him completely, she couldn't quite understand why he'd spoken in Russian.

Interpreting her confusion, the man pressed on. *'Je suis désolé, vous m'avez surpris.'*

He smiled apologetically, as if this strange encounter were his fault and not hers for walking through the woods at some awful hour of the morning dressed in…dressed in… Oh, God! Ella almost groaned, but turned it into a rueful laugh.

'Perhaps we could continue in English, if you speak it. It's been a…long day.'

'It is only six o'clock in the morning, so I must assume a *very* long day.' He looked her over and she suddenly realised that he could quite easily misinterpret the reason for her appearance, which made her think of all the reasons she *was* in the woods in a ball gown and red velvet cape after spending twelve hours by her grandmother's bedside.

The forest's dew had soaked into the cloak and, more than its heaviness, she now felt cold. Cold and hungry and tired. But as she began to shiver she realised that it was not from the damp or the temperature, but the effect of being this man's sole focus.

'Where are you going?' he asked gently, as if not wanting to scare her further.

'My grandmother's house. It's just up the path and not far.'

She braced herself as Dorcas leaned into her, almost at waist height.

'Dorcas!' the man almost growled at his dog in warning, yet the dog only answered with a playful yip before collapsing in a heap at Ella's feet and showing her belly as if to say, *Here. Rub here.*

'Stop flirting, Dorcas,' came her owner's somewhat exasperated response as he tucked the lead he'd been holding into the pocket of his wax jacket.

Ella couldn't help but smile at the interaction and it felt almost strange and unfamiliar on features that had felt so weighed down by worry and stress. She bent down to rub the massive beast at her feet and laughed as she realised that Dorcas had trapped her cloak beneath her and effectively pinned her in place.

But in truth she felt more trapped by the steady gaze of the man whose name she still did not know.

'Out past your curfew?' he asked.

'I… I was at a party in Moscow when I got a phone call to say that my grandmother had been taken to hospital.'

His frown deepened and for a heartbeat Ella wondered what he might look like when not frowning. She could sense a barrage of questions building between them but he asked the most important.

'Is she okay?'

'I don't know,' she replied honestly, catching a moment of concern in his stunning eyes before something fell over them, closing off whatever she might have seen there.

'Are *you*?' he asked. Incapable of answering that question, of putting words to whatever it was she was currently feeling, she shook her head. 'We're going that way if you would like the company?' the beast's owner pressed on.

Dorcas elegantly leapt from the forest floor as if punctuating her master's query with excitement and joy, bringing yet another unfamiliar smile to Ella's features.

'Yes, that would be nice,' she replied truthfully, and suddenly she felt she might buckle under the exhaustion she'd held at bay for the last twelve hours.

'Roman,' he said, holding out his hand.

'Ella,' she replied and felt a jolt of electricity snap

through her body from where her hand met his. He laid his other hand on top as if holding hers in place when she would have pulled away and, rather than feeling uncertain or awkward, she simply felt…safe.

The short journey to her grandmother's cottage passed almost in silence and Ella found herself unusually at peace in Roman's company.

They came to the edge of the forest and followed a dirt track leading towards the little chocolate box cottage that Ella loved so much. Her hand naturally went out to caress the small stone pillars either side of the short driveway, as she did every single time she came here. Almost on autopilot, she went to the large, worn wooden door and pushed it open— her grandmother never having once locked the entrance to her home. She led her strange procession of Roman and Dorcas into the house, and stopped the moment she saw the foot of the stairs where her grandmother had fallen and lain for hours before being found.

A shiver cut through her body and she had to fight hard against the urge to cry in front of a stranger who did not feel like a stranger.

The cottage was cast in darkness, the thin light in the centre of the front room doing little to dispel the early morning shadows, and she stood, blankly staring ahead until she realised that she was looking straight at Roman who, once again, seemed greatly concerned about her.

He nodded to himself once, as if coming to a decision, and turned towards the fireplace and set about building a fire from the logs and kindling beside it. All the while she stood there as if capable of no more. She certainly felt that way.

Once the fire was crackling and snapping, beautiful flames dancing and reaching towards the open damper, he came towards her and stood so close that she had to lift her head up to see his face. Some wicked sense within her wanted to lean into him. Wanted him to take her in his arms. As if sensing her thoughts, he lifted his hands.

'May I?'

She wasn't sure what he was asking for but nodded her permission anyway. She feared for a moment that she would give this stranger anything. A numbness had settled about her and she felt detached from the world about her but deeply present for the man in front of her.

His hands came together to release the clasp holding the cloak about her shoulders, and gently pushed it back and placed it aside. She shivered at the brief contact of his hands against her skin, the low neckline of her dress leaving her vulnerable to his touch. Her pulse kicked up and goose bumps prickled her skin as he guided her to the sofa opposite the fire and placed a warm cashmere blanket around her shoulders.

'Is there anyone I can call for you?'

'No.'

He seemed displeased by this answer, as if outraged by the thought of her being alone. Leaving her in the living area, he disappeared from sight and she heard the sounds of a kettle being boiled, cups and spoons being rattled and the fridge opening and closing.

When he returned to her, she marvelled at the lack of fear she felt as he loomed over her. No, most definitely not fear, but a strange yearning even she could recognise was outrageously inappropriate. Inexplicably, she wanted to reach for him, to steal some of the strength she could almost feel emanating from him.

In spite of the darkness of the cottage, Ella saw the molten heat in his eyes, felt it warm her more than any fire or flame. Heard the sharp intake of his breath, and watched with a sense of shame as he stepped back from her. Her cheeks burnt and she turned her head aside, hoping that she hadn't betrayed herself, as a curl of confused humiliation swept through her.

'I should go.'

This drew her gaze back to his, now completely shadowed by the shafts of shade in the cottage.

'How can I thank you?'

'We can figure that out next time.'

'Next time?' Ella repeated, hating that she sounded so hopeful.

'The next time we meet in the woods.'

* * *

It was two days before she saw any sign of Roman again. Two days in which her grandmother regained consciousness and underwent operations and procedures to heal her hip and the shoulder fracture resulting from the fall.

When her grandmother had first woken, she had mistaken Ella for her mother, Adeline. It had only been for a few moments, but the bittersweet cut to her heart had been deep. Her grandmother was Ella's only connection to her French mother and she hoarded any fragments Claudette had ever told her. Ella's childhood summers had been spent wandering the woods and delving deeper into the stories that her grandmother would tell of the handsome American tycoon Nathaniel Riding and the sweet innocent Adeline Ardoin who had met, fallen in love and married within months. She knew her grandmother had been heartbroken when they had relocated to Russia for Nathaniel's business and even more lost when Adeline had passed away, and Ella had been reluctant to break the spell that had returned Claudette's daughter to her, almost sixteen years after her death.

But her grandmother's sharp mind had quickly orientated itself and, with a single tear slowly tumbling down her softly lined features, Claudette Ardoin had shaken her head and apologised for being an old fool. After several meetings with doctors and medical personnel, it was clear that Claudette would be staying in hospital for at least two weeks and was highly unlikely to be able to return to the cottage and her independence that she valued so much.

It was the awful practicalities, the decisions to be made, the almost upsetting specifics of moving her grandmother into a care home that left Ella feeling a little shaken and unsettled. And with startling clarity she realised the magnitude of what her guardian had done for her as a child.

When her parents had been killed in a helicopter accident, Ella had been only five. Even all those years ago, Claudette had not been able to take her in and care for her, due to her age and minimal income, and Ella had been given over to Vladimir Kolikov, her father's business partner and closest friend. So the daughter of an American father—an only son whose parents had both died far too young—and a French mother went to live in Russia with a man who might have been a bit isolated and cold, but was more than ready and willing to give her a home, to care for her and make decisions for her. Vladimir was not the easiest of men, but Ella felt an affection there and as a child had split her time between boarding school in Switzerland, summers in France and winters in Russia.

As she prepared to leave the cottage to return to the hospital, she wondered at meeting Roman—who she had thought of a lot in the last two days. At the peculiarity of meeting a Russian in the deepest part of the South of France. Perhaps that was why she felt there was something slightly similar between her guardian and her rescuer, as she had come to think of him.

And once again she felt the painful blush of embarrassment sting her cheeks. Roman must have thought her completely incompetent. A woman who allowed a stranger into her home, watched in silence as he built a fire, made sure there was food in the fridge and went so far as to set out the makings of a cup of tea. A woman who wanted…things she should not, she concluded to herself as she grabbed her bag and opened the front door.

It was then that she saw the small parcel on the top of the steps. Casting a glance out into the woods, she saw nothing but swathes of trees with windswept leaves, enticingly cool shadowed pathways and long stretches of bluebells.

Returning her attention to the lavender-coloured tissue paper bound with brown string, she picked it up and saw a small cream tag with small, neat writing in English.

To replace what was lost.

Frowning, she picked the bow of the string apart and carefully unwrapped the package in case it might have somehow come by accident to the wrong house. The paper parted to reveal a swathe of burgundy, the softest cashmere she had ever touched. She drew out the present and marvelled at the floor-length hooded cape, by far superior to the one that had been all but destroyed by her journey through the woods two days ago.

It was exquisite and could only have come from one person. Her fingers ran down the stunning material and she was overwhelmed by the gift. Felt a heady combination of joy, surprise and excitement that Roman had thought of her and given her such a gift. Wearing it, she knew, would make her feel beautiful…but also strangely guilty. A guilty pleasure that was only surpassed by the hope that she would see him again. Soon.

Roman reluctantly turned away from the sight of Ella on the doorstep to her grandmother's cottage. Even as everything in him wanted to consume whatever sight of her he could, he ruthlessly thrust aside his base desires in favour of his true intention. He felt every inch the predator he had been forced to become to reach his desired goal. It was imprinted on his soul—it had shaped him, directed him for so many years and now vengeance was within his grasp.

He had been shocked by her innocence. Truly. Expecting to find Vladimir's ward hardened, sharp with angles by her time spent with such an evil man, instead he'd wondered at the untouched quality of her. She had, two days ago, seemed like a fairy-tale creature. It had made him forget his purpose. As if she had some magical power that had made him almost forget everything. He'd not missed how she had looked at him in the cottage. When the cashmere cloak had half slipped from her shoulder, revealing the curve of pale skin, he'd struggled with the urge to draw her near. He hadn't missed the way her pupils had dilated, casting her inky blue eyes in an unfathomable dark hue that spoke of desire and want.

Nor had he missed the blush of embarrassment as if she did not know what she was wanting. And it had been that which had broken the spell.

Her beauty was undeniable and he acknowledged, reluctantly, the small part of him that wished perhaps that things were different. But they were not. He had set about this path the moment Vladimir had signed his mother's death warrant eighteen years ago.

Searing pain gripped him hard and fast, taking him by surprise and shocking him with its intensity. A thick, heavy grief-laden nausea swirled in his gut as if he felt that terrible blow for the first time. The horrifying blankness that had descended once he'd felt the bewildering impossibility of moving forward, of surviving without the one person in his life who had anchored him, who had loved him. It had crashed over him like a wave he hadn't already surfed. Roman struggled to breathe and forced the pressure in his chest to morph from grief to fury in a years-old practised technique.

Fury at the memory of his grandfather refusing the pleas of a thirteen-year-old boy, begging for help, for finances that would pay for the medical treatment his mother so desperately needed. Vladimir had slammed the door on him. And the consequences had been devastating.

Now Kolikov would know that same feeling. Roman wanted Vladimir to beg and plead as he had once done. Ella Riding was the *only* way he could take revenge against his grandfather. And he would take it by any means necessary.

CHAPTER TWO

There are many forms of disguise, some in clothing, some in nature, but the most dangerous of all are those that have the thread of truth stitched through them, making it even harder to pull truth from fiction.
        The Truth About Little Red Riding Hood
                    —Roz Fayrer

EVER SINCE SHE had come to France, time had seemed to lose all meaning for Ella. Hours spent with her grandmother passed in a second—as if knowing it was running out, time raced headlong towards an impossible finish line. Yet mere moments spent with Roman seemed to draw out deliciously as if he held as much command over the grains of sand in an hourglass as he did over her body and senses.

But, more than that, in the last month he had become her confidant, her support. She had spoken to Vladimir on the phone, but his lack of interest in her maternal grandmother had left her feeling strangely awkward and isolated. Despite the initial fear for her health, the procedures and operations had gone incredibly well. But that relief had been short-lived as Ella suddenly found herself the only person who could, and had to, make decisions about care homes and closing up Claudette's long-lived life in the cottage.

Ella would have found it all too much to bear had it not been for Roman. He had listened to her fears, helped her talk through the visiting of various homes, advised her on how to approach her grandmother with the best on offer. Her grandmother's pension didn't cover anywhere near the amount needed and Ella had been forced to ask Vladimir for an advance on her trust fund from her parents. At the age of twenty-two, she was three years away from full access to it and the monthly stipend that had seemed more than enough simply wouldn't stretch to the beautiful care home she had found for Claudette. Only an hour away from Toulouse, it might have seemed like an extravagance—as suggested by Vladimir, who couldn't understand why 'the old crone' couldn't be left to public health care—but Ella simply couldn't wrench her grandmother away from the looming view of the Pyrenees that she had seen every morning since birth.

Ella had been surprised when Roman had happily put aside his business interests in the area to focus almost all his fierce attention on supporting her. Never before had she experienced such a thing and if she had been concerned with how quickly and how fast her dependence on him had come into her life she thrust it aside. Daily walks with Roman and Dorcas had kept her sane and forced her out of the cottage she would have sunk into and never left. Those walks had turned into evening meals where Roman would pepper her with questions about her life in seductive tones and with enticing smiles.

'So, tell me. What was little Ella Riding like?'

She spent hours sharing tales of her boarding school life, her hopes for the future, plans that she had only begun to discuss with her friend Célia. The business they wanted to develop by linking powerful industries and rich investors with charities across the globe. The home that Ella wanted one day. Roman had listened, smiling and laughing, and encouraging her fantasies of what it would look like, how many rooms, bathrooms, and how much land she would like. He had seemed to sense how important it was to her when she had tried to convey how difficult it had been growing up and feeling as if she'd never had a home of her own—her time shared between her boarding school, university, her guardian's estate in Russia and her grandmother's cottage here in France. All of which were welcoming and wonderful, but never truly hers and hers alone.

Once her grandmother had begun to rally, she and Roman began to wander further afield than the woods surrounding the cottage. It was only when she had arrived at the small airfield where a private jet waited to whisk them away to Paris for the evening that Ella realised that Roman was more than just a man of means, but someone really quite incredibly wealthy.

She was no stranger to money and had always lived with the knowledge that at the age of twenty-five she would inherit a vast trust fund from her parents. But, until that time, anything she needed had always had to be approved by her guardian or come from the somewhat conservative monthly allowance he had provided for her from that trust fund. And ever since completing her degree, ever since her return to France, Ella had begun to strain a little at the leash, envying Roman his complete freedom and control over his own destiny.

But as they had flown to Paris in Roman's private plane, as they had sat in the exquisite restaurant encased within the Eiffel Tower, a landmark Roman had mocked her for not visiting before, she had realised that for all that she had shared of herself, she knew very little about the tall, impossibly handsome man who made her heart soar and her pulse race.

'So, Roman Black. Who are you really?'

He'd explained in broad terms and simple descriptions that he hadn't always been wealthy, and that he had had to fight to get everything he now had. Her heart had burned with sympathy as he'd roughly told her of his mother's death when he was thirteen, and they had shared a sense of that impossible to describe feeling that descended when everything you thought you knew changed in a heartbeat. Ella might have been only five when her parents had died, but she knew what it was like to have the rug pulled from beneath your feet, to lose that precious mooring— the absolute conviction that your parents were there and would always love and care for you.

She had been impressed by the man who had managed to turn everything around against all possible hope and grow into a kind and generous, patient man who she couldn't help but build dreams around. So she could be forgiven, perhaps, for failing to realise that, once again, Roman had turned the conversation back to her before it became too focused on himself.

Trips to Paris were soon followed by visits to London and Stockholm, never too far from an easy return to her grandmother should anything have gone awry. But it never did and soon Ella had begun to relax into this strange new world at which Roman was the centre.

Only her friend Célia had provided words of caution—fearing that perhaps it was all a little too soon, too much. *'What do you know about him?'* she had asked over the phone. *'Enough,'* had been Ella's determined reply.

She knew how Roman made her feel, she knew how Roman had made her want. Want more, not only

for herself, but for him too. And her untried and un-
tested heart blossomed beneath his every attention.
Her feelings were even more assured once Roman
had met Claudette, causing Ella to believe that, had
her grandmother been several decades younger, she
too would have fallen under his spell.

Claudette's joy that Ella might have found the
same fairy-tale romance as her daughter once had
with Nathaniel Riding only served to signpost to Ella
that she was indeed on the right path. That of happiness and true love. In some small way, it touched
Ella that she was echoing her mother's life. That, like
Adeline, she had met and fallen in love with the man
of her dreams. It made her feel connected to both her
mother and the past in a way that she couldn't have
imagined only a month before.

So when, only a week ago, Roman had revealed
that he was needed back in Russia within a fortnight,
Ella's heart had beat and pulsed with a pre-emptive
agony and she had vainly struggled to hide the tears
that had unexpectedly gathered.

He had swept aside one with the pad of his thumb
and pressed the sweetest kiss against her lips. A kiss
that had built a storm of need and passion within her
as if, so desperate to cling to him, to keep him with
her, she would have given him anything. She *wanted*
to give him *everything*.

However, Roman had been steadfast on this one
thing. A deeply traditional man, he believed that only

her husband should have that right, and his declaration had served only to make him seem even more perfect in her eyes, no matter how much she wanted to dissuade him of his conviction.

That night, when he had left, she had been bereft. It was as if that simple declaration of what could be between them, but wasn't, had made her consumed with the desire to be his wife. It invaded her thoughts and heart with an insidiousness that Ella, in her naivety, believed was nothing less than true love.

So that when they had next met, when he had whisked her away to a candlelit dinner in a chateau overlooking the dips and swells of the rolling hillside, peppered with small terracotta towns and church towers and sprawling vineyards, she had seen nothing but the look of love in his eyes as he haltingly, almost hesitantly, admitted that he knew it was soon, knew it was quick, but he couldn't remain quiet any longer. That he wanted her to be his wife, his love, his companion. She had almost interrupted his proposal with an agreement so ready, so earnest he had smiled and produced the most beautiful ring she had ever seen.

The art deco ring—a ruby encased in diamonds, set on dual silver bands which were, in turn, covered in more diamonds—looked as if it had come from her deepest fantasies. Roman had explained that ever since their first meeting in the woods he had imagined her in red. And it had touched Ella deeply that he too must have felt all that she had, from the first moment they had met.

But still his departure from France loomed over them. It was only when she shared her joyful news with Claudette that Ella saw and felt her every desire was achievable. Her grandmother's insistence that she be freed from her caregiver duties gave Ella hope. But it also made her want to give something back in return. She knew in that moment that nothing less than having her grandmother present on her wedding day would make her the happiest bride in the world. Hoping beyond all hope that Roman would agree, she hesitantly broached her request to marry before he needed to return to Russia. His agreement was immediate and assured. But he had a request of his own—one that touched her very soul. Knowing how important her guardian was to her, he wished to return to Moscow on the eve of their nuptials and pay respect to the man who had given her so much.

So overwhelmed that he would consider her wants and needs, the small smattering of people she classed as family, soon to be stretched to include one more, Ella didn't give much thought to what would happen next. Roman had already given her so much that she placed her trust and her future in his hands. A future he seemed to consider a little more than herself, for he presented her with a prenup, insisting her future and her father's inheritance was and would always be hers, protected by the agreement he wanted her to sign, despite the fact she would willingly have not. It was as if he had thought of everything, and in those thoughts had put her first and foremost. And to a young woman who had always felt as if she owed a debt, to either her guardian or grandmother, it was everything.

And as she stood before the closed wooden door of the church she chose not to focus on the fact she hadn't called Célia to tell her of the wedding, nor that her closest friend wasn't even there. Ella felt strongly that Célia wouldn't have understood, hadn't even when she'd tried before to tell her how much Roman meant to her. Instead, Ella chose to defiantly remain in this little bubble world that she had created for herself and Roman.

Her pulse picked up as she cast one final glance in the floor-length mirror discreetly tucked away behind a pillar. She ran a hand down the smooth oyster-coloured silk dress that fitted her perfectly, simple but delicate silver and pearl beading detailing the plunging neckline between her small breasts and the fabric sweeping over slightly flared hips down to her ankles.

Ella hadn't noticed the split in the skirts until she'd first tried it on and walked towards the reflection in the mirror of her grandmother's cottage. Never before had she worn such a thing, but she couldn't shake the feeling that somehow a fairy godmother was looking over her. But it wasn't a character from

some long-ago-written fairy tale but her mother who
had kept the beautiful gown for her daughter to wear
one day. And Ella believed it was yet another sign
as she stood in her mother's wedding dress, about to
marry the man of her dreams.

Everything was proceeding as planned. Better than
Roman could have ever hoped, in fact. In the last
month he had played his part well. And if somewhere deep within his soul his conscience thrashed,
he ruthlessly thrust it aside, focusing instead on the
end goal.

But strangely, as he stood at the top of the aisle
of the small church with domed ceilings and faded
frescos, as he smiled at Claudette, who already had
a handkerchief pressed to the corners of her eyes,
in the pews with only two others—neighbours who
had known Ella since she was a child—acting as wit-
nesses, he felt unease stirring in his chest.

Roman had no intention of making this marriage
real. He was a monster, but not so much of one that
he would take her innocence. He was sure that Vladimir would agree to his demands and the marriage
would be annulled almost as quickly as it would take
for Ella to say, *I do*. But, in spite of that mental assurance to himself, the small ceremony felt…more
real than anything had for a long time.

A small whine from the floor drew his attention
to Dorcas. The priest had been a little dubious about

the prospect of having an animal in attendance, but Ella had insisted. Roman was half convinced that she loved the dog as much as she appeared to have fallen in love with her fiancé. Thinking of himself in the third person in relation to Ella had been almost the only way to isolate himself from her effect.

It had been Ella's fiancé who had whisked her away to Paris. Ella's fiancé who had listened to her hopes and dreams and Ella's fiancé who had believed very strongly in the sanctity of marriage. For if it had been Roman himself, he would have devoured her completely on that very first day and ruined the only bargaining chip he had with Vladimir.

Roman had always marvelled at the value placed on a woman's innocence. Yet in the month that he had worked hard to preserve Ella's, for her own sake as much as his, he had begun to understand the fascination and had happily consigned his frustrated desire for her as the price he had to pay for his vengeance.

Dorcas whined again from where she sat by his feet, and stared up at him as if questioning whether he knew what he was doing. He frowned at the dog, a dominant warning growl threatening to rumble in his throat, and finally she turned her attention back to the church door as if knowing Ella stood on the other side.

And Roman couldn't help but be curious as to what those doors would reveal when they parted, excusing the sense of all-consuming anticipation as mild interest rather than the raging beast of desire. He had offered to arrange for her to go to Paris in search of a wedding dress, but she had smiled and simply stated that she had it *'covered'*.

Simple. On the surface that was what Ella seemed to be, but over the last few weeks he had realised that she was nothing of the sort. In an odd way, getting to know her had been like watching someone grow into themselves. Evolve, develop, try and test things out, ideas and hopes and dreams. All the things he had never been able to do himself, after being thrust into adulthood at the age of thirteen when his mother had died. The hardships and devastation of the following years as he had been moved from foster home to foster home, working any part-time job he could, saving every single penny for the university education he knew he would need if he was ever to get himself to a rich enough position to be able to get his revenge. Determination as much as a shockingly intense intellect had been all he'd needed to succeed.

That and an almost preternatural ability to identify what it was that a person most wanted in this world.

At school, his stature and intellect had seemed to entice weak-minded bullies who sought to either befriend or remove a possible threat to their power. But Roman had never entertained their games, nor had he existed within any specific circle—instead staying on the fringes, a lone wolf, ready and able to befriend or berate as suited his own personal needs. For he had learned at a young age that true power was about dependence and manipulation. Getting someone to willingly hand over what it was he wanted was far more valuable than coercion.

And as he grew older, through university and the following years building up a personal empire that made him one of the richest men in the western hemisphere, he had used that skill very well indeed. He had amassed a vast property empire, including a number of highly sought after and deeply exclusive nightclubs, but his true skill lay in brokering hugely successful business deals for others...at an eye-wateringly high price of course. His telephone contact list boasted several royals and world leaders on speed dial, more than a few oligarchs, and one or two more nefarious characters.

But, in spite of this, his one goal was Kolikov Holdings. It was his mother's birthright, had her own father not cast her aside the moment she had failed to give in to his wishes and marry Nathaniel Riding. Instead, she had fallen in love with a weak-minded carpenter who had been bought off by Vladimir the moment he had discovered Tatiana's unmarried pregnancy. As she had refused to give in to her father's demands and terminate her child, Vladimir had severed all ties to his daughter and grandchild, emotional and financial. And Roman would make sure that he would pay for his actions.

The way he had felt when he had first realised that

Ella had replaced his mother's position had been as if his heart were gripped in a steel vice. In fact, it had been as the door had slammed on his face when he had begged and pleaded with Vladimir to provide the necessary finances to fund his mother's treatment that he had first laid eyes on her. A little blonde girl of five years, hair curling around chubby cheeks and little fists grabbing for toys, the like of which Roman had never seen before in his life. He had ducked behind the bushes that lined his grandfather's estate in Moscow and watched in rage as this little girl played happily with all the things that he and his mother had been denied. It had not taken much investigation to discover the story of the daughter who had been presented to Vladimir as his ward, nor had it taken long to realise that she was presently enjoying a life that should have been his mother's.

And while he acknowledged that he could not place the blame for this at her feet, over the next few years he realised that Ella had become the apple of his grandfather's eye. The one and only object of sentiment the old man seemed to possess, aside from his precious Kolikov Holdings. And while the bastard had shored up any and all attempts to breach the impenetrable walls around his company, Roman had marvelled at how the man had somehow managed to leave his ward so utterly vulnerable in this world.

Vladimir had seemed to delight in showing off the exquisitely beautiful trophy child at the Russian Debutante ball in London, or presenting her at some high-profile gala across the globe, and every picture, every newspaper article only twisted the knife deeper and confirmed his conviction that she was the only way to truly get what he wanted: Vladimir to hand over control of the company that should be Roman's by right. Vladimir to pass ownership to the man he'd called a worthless bastard, good for nothing more than begging for scraps from a man who would rather cut his own nose off than acknowledge Roman's legitimacy. And once Roman had control of that company he would tear it apart piece by piece right in front of Kolikov.

The creak of the large wooden door at the bottom of the church drew Roman's thoughts back to the present. There she was. The key to his revenge. He was sure that it was that knowledge that made his heart leap in his chest—not the stunning sight of the lamb about to be sacrificed on the altar of his revenge.

Ella was dressed in an oyster silk dress, simple lines clinging to a figure most women would have paid thousands of euros to achieve. The low V of the dress moulded to Ella's perfect frame and his heart beat a powerful tattoo that he was too stunned to fight. Something primal roared within him. Need and want a heady combination that burned through his veins and his soul. But he'd sold his soul long ago and couldn't turn back now—no matter how much he might want to.

He felt his pupils widen as if trying to take as

much in of the image of Ella before him. As if trying desperately to consume every single detail of this moment. And, for some inexplicable reason, he felt as if it would be his last. Because after this moment, after they said *I do*, it would all change. Because the moment she discovered the truth she would hate him with every fibre of her being, and he would deserve it.

In some twisted way, his inner voice lashed at those thoughts in self-defence.

Better she finds out now what Vladimir is like. What I am like. Because her innocence, her naivety, won't get her far in this life.

Just like it hadn't for him or his mother.

But as the words of the priest washed over him, joining them as husband and wife, as the music played to signal the end of the service and he was directed to kiss his bride, Roman lost all thought of revenge, of the separate person who had married Ella Riding, of his promise to leave her untouched. Instead he focused on the soft lips parting beneath his—the gentle, sweet sweep of Ella's tongue as she opened for him, as she enticed him further into her depths. He lost his head and drew her to him, heedless of the gentle laughter of the few others in the small church, and wished that it could be different.

Reluctantly he pulled back, because it wasn't different, and he wasn't. The only gift he could give her on her wedding day would be to leave her unsullied by his touch. Even if it nearly killed him.

CHAPTER THREE

*She had stalked his woods and haunted his
dreams. She had strayed from the path...and
now she was his, to do with as he wished.*
The Truth About Little Red Riding Hood
—Roz Fayrer

MARRIED. SHE WAS MARRIED. Ella pressed her fingers
to her lips, still thrumming from the kiss that had
sealed her fate. There had been kisses between them
before—of course there had—but nothing compared
to the searing passion she'd felt almost consuming
her the moment he'd claimed her before the priest
and God. Ever since, her body had been in a constant state of awareness, soaring between hot and
cold, both of which produced goose bumps across
her skin, prickles of need and want. Heat coiled low
within her and nothing would satiate it. Certainly
not the hooded glances she felt from Roman when
he thought she was not looking.

Barely two hours ago, she had bid her grand-

mother *adieu* and been whisked away in Roman's
private jet and now they were en route to Belarus.
It seemed impossible to her that she had taken the
reverse of this same journey only five weeks ago.
Then she had been filled with fear for her grandmother, feeling impossibly lonely and helpless. Yet
now her grandmother was safe and happy, and she
was about to embark on a new life with a man who
filled her days with joy and made her feel…strong?
Capable? Even as she thought it, she shushed a very
Célia-sounding voice chiding that she shouldn't need
a man to make her feel those things.

'Can I get you anything?' asked the perfectly presented male attendant.

She smiled and shook her head, half fearful that
she would blurt out that she needed no more than
what she now had in her life. All that was left to do
before she could truly begin was for Roman to meet
Vladimir, and then… She frowned. They hadn't actually discussed where they would go after that meeting. She'd been so focused on actually getting to the
wedding, thoughts and discussions of what would
happen next had seemed almost impossible.

Now, sitting on the plane, she realised it was almost silly not to know where she was going. And it
both excited her and made her a little uncomfortable.
She had placed all of her trust in Roman. He would
look after her, she knew it. But as she cast a glance
at her husband, who had spent a large portion of the

flight so far consumed by whatever he was reading on his tablet, that unease began to grow.

He was unusually quiet, and Dorcas seemed to pick up on this too as she padded between them, back and forth across the aisle of the small cabin. Dorcas hmphed down into a shape the size of a giant boulder at her feet and Ella didn't have the heart to be worried about her dress. The warmth and physical contact was a balm to her heightened senses.

She caressed the wiry tendrils beneath Dorcas's jaw and large yellow eyes stared up at her as if in concern. Strangely, she found herself reassuring the animal as much as herself with gently whispered words so as not to disturb Roman's concentration.

'Is everything okay?' she finally ventured after another half an hour of silence.

'*Da.*'

It was strange hearing Roman speak Russian. Even though Ella was fluent, they had always reverted to English. But from the moment they'd stepped onto the plane, all of Roman's directions to the pilot and the staff had been in Russian, even the few sentences he had shared with her. As if he had forgotten the way things had been between them for the last month.

'Are you nervous?' she asked, hoping that might be the reason for the strange mood that had descended over her husband.

At this, he finally put aside his phone and looked at her with some confusion. 'Why would I be nervous?'

'About meeting my guardian. I know your businesses are in a different area, but Kolikov is a fairly well-known name and I'm aware that he has…a reputation.'

Roman smiled—a smile that Ella had not seen from him before. *Predatory*. The word ran through her mind before she could stop it.

'No. In fact, I am relishing it.'

His response did nothing to appease the concern rising within her breast and suddenly she longed to call Célia. To tell her about her marriage, to hear words of reassurance that Ella couldn't be sure would be forthcoming. Her mind became unaccountably blank, as if choosing to think of nothing rather than the fears that were brewing.

In a limousine, they travelled stretches of tarmac drawing them away from the small private airfield outside of Moscow towards Vladimir's estate. Roman's usually single-minded focus was fractured. As much as he tried to force his thoughts to his goal, he couldn't rid himself of the awareness of his bride. He could sense her withdrawal—one of his own making. He knew that his curt answers and almost brutal brooding had affected her.

It both was and wasn't intentional, for he no longer needed the pretence of the doting husband. He had what he wanted—the key to his revenge. Now he just had to turn the key in the lock. Everything in his life since the age of thirteen had been about this moment. Every dark thing he'd ever done, educational achievement, business deal, his sole focus had been leading to this point.

He'd identified Ella as the only thing that Vladimir cared about other than his company. He'd watched from afar, seeing how Ella was showered with everything that his mother had not been. Suddenly he felt a surge of resentment towards her, knowing that to be unfair. It wasn't her fault, but she was connected to that man's world—her ignorance was no excuse. But, if Vladimir gave him everything he wanted, then perhaps she might escape with as little hurt as possible.

If Vladimir gave him the company that was his by right, to do with as he wished, to destroy in front of the very man whose sole focus had excluded his daughter, then Roman would retreat from Ella's life—leaving her untouched and their wedding annulled. She might never even know the true depth of his actions.

But only if Vladimir had even an ounce of sentiment towards the girl. Roman hoped he did. For her sake.

Roman found it strange that he recognised the roads leading towards the estate. As if everything about that day, all those years ago, had been indelibly printed on his soul. The way the sun had beat down on him for every single one of the twenty minutes it had taken him to walk from where the bus had stopped. The way his chest had ached from leaving his mother behind and spending the precious little time they had left on his quest. The way his rough clothes had felt against his skin. The way that hope had bloomed in his chest as he felt convinced that the old man would repent, would save his mother.

The slice of devastation, humiliation and agony that had torn through him as the door had been slammed in his face was still fresh. As was the bitterness and anger he'd seen in the old man's eyes, the resentment. That was the night Roman had been truly born.

As they passed through wrought-iron gates Roman remembered Ella asking him on the plane if everything was okay. Now he mentally answered that it was *more* than okay. That it was perfect.

As they drew to a stop, Ella almost excitedly launched herself out of the limousine. She had decided that once they got this meeting out of the way, everything would go back to how it had been before. That the man she had fallen in love with would return to her, and she would never see this dark, brooding wolfish figure again. Dorcas loped along beside her and if Konstantin—her guardian's housekeeper—thought anything strange about the presence of the animal he was too well trained to say.

Kissing the gruff man on the cheek, she blindly grasped Roman's hand and hurried into the mansion before she could see Konstantin's dark look at the man she had married. As always when she entered the sprawling entrance hall, she was stunned by the marble flooring and sweeping spiral staircase in the corner, the grandeur nothing like what little she remembered of her one-time childhood home with her parents. Releasing Roman's hand, she gave in to the desire for her childhood ritual of spinning in a circle in the centre of the hall. It had started as a way to stop from buckling beneath the awe of it all, the unfamiliarity of it, and Ella suddenly found she needed it now. A self-conscious giggle rose up in her chest at her own silliness as she drew to a halt, expecting to see Roman's soft indulgent, understanding smile that she had grown to depend upon. But instead he was looking about him as if disappointed.

'He is in a meeting, miss, and asked that you wait for him in the living room.'

Thrusting aside her fears, Ella instead reached once again for Roman's hand and drew him towards the room indicated by Konstantin. She chose to cling to the threads of her own happiness. A happiness she hadn't realised was missing from her life before Roman. She'd been going through the motions at school and university, Ella had realised. The roughly sketched-out company she'd been talking to Célia about just a way to pass the time. But now Ella was about to start a new chapter in her life. As a woman. As a wife. As someone in her own right. All this joy she desperately clung to, ignoring the fact that Roman's hand had slipped from hers.

She turned to find him pouring himself a drink from the small bar area and felt oddly disquieted by the way he seemed to feel so at home in a room she had never really liked. As if it was his. As if he had the right. It was such a contrast to the almost humble man she had come to know. The arrogance somehow made her feel embarrassed on his behalf as Konstantin took in the same action with something like disdain.

'Would you care for a drink?' The simple request had come from her guardian's housekeeper, not her husband, making it almost impossible for Ella to ignore that something was wrong. Very wrong.

'I think that would be a good idea,' came a gravelly voice behind her. 'I have a feeling she's going to need it.'

She turned to find her guardian looming in the shadows cast from the doorway to the hall. The smile on her lips wavered at Vladimir's proclamation. Even though he was nearing eighty, her guardian had always stood tall and proud. Stocky rather than softly rounded, and always shockingly dark-featured compared to her pale skin and blonde hair from her mother's side. He had always seemed formidable to her but now, here, he felt almost menacing.

'So this is the man you have married?' he demanded as he stepped into the room. The Russian words were harsh against her heart in comparison to the month spent with the softer, warmer French of her grandmother.

'Yes,' she said, looking back at her husband, hoping to have him stand by her side, but feeling an unbreachable distance between them across the room. 'Please let me introduce Roman Black. My husband.'

'Black?' queried her guardian. 'Not a surname I'm familiar with.'

Vladimir's gaze bored into Roman's unrelentingly. And Ella wondered why the man who had charmed her, who had eased her grandmother's concerns aside with smooth words and confidences, was not now attempting to do the same with her guardian. Instead, he appeared as if carved from stone, holding fast against the battering winds being thrown in his direction by Vladimir Kolikov.

It was as if the temperature in the room had dropped, a hostility she had never before felt covering her skin in goose bumps.

'I would like a moment with your new husband, Ella.'

The dismissal was perhaps not unusual, but most unexpected. She was about to protest, but one quick glare from Vladimir cut the words before they could form. Roman had yet to take his eyes from her guardian and Ella felt as if she were at sea, being pushed and pulled by invisible currents that she let carry her from the room.

But she refused to be so easily dismissed and instead paused in the hallway, leaving the door ever so slightly ajar.

'You said you would be back.'

Ella frowned from where she stood, hidden in the shadows beside the door. Roman knew her guardian?

'I did,' Roman replied, his voice almost unrecognisable.

'And you have married my ward.'

'I have.'

'To what end?'

'That is entirely dependent on you, Kolikov.'

Ella struggled to understand what was going on. The words she could hear as easily as if had she been in the room, but the meaning? It was completely lost on her. The shifting sand beneath her feet made her feel nauseous as she struggled to wrap her head around the conversation taking place through the door. Her heart beat fiercely against the invisible threat that hovered above her like a sword.

'Why Black?'

'What?'

'The name. Why Black?'

'It was the colour my heart turned when you kicked me off your property. It was the depth of the darkness my heart became when she died.'

'I see you are just as fanciful as that girl.'

'That girl was your *daughter*!' Roman raged and in that moment an overwhelming force of horror struck Ella hard and fast. Roman was Vladimir's grandson?

'She stopped being my daughter the day she chose you over me,' the old man spat.

'Well, now this is *your* choice. *Your* reckoning.'

'Really? Pray tell.'

'I have what you value most in this world. I wouldn't say love, because clearly you are not capable of such a thing. Or perhaps that is reserved only for your company. Either way, now you must choose. You can hand over control and ownership of Kolikov Holdings and I will let her go. The marriage will be annulled. Or—' Roman paused, as if ensuring he had the man's complete attention '—I will leave Ella Riding ruined and destitute, just like my mother was.'

Ella's legs buckled as she pressed a hand to her mouth to stifle the moan that threatened to escape her lips. It had all been lies? Every touch, every kiss, every word… Her heart severed from its moorings, cut through with a knife so sharp she felt flayed. Her husband was threatening to ruin her. The man she had fallen in love with, the man she had naively entrusted her future to. Bile rose in the back of her throat as she see-sawed between feeling devastating betrayal and hoping against hope that her guardian would come to her rescue. Would somehow defeat the beast that she had unwittingly married.

Later she would wonder whether she should have gone, fled the estate then. But if she had she would never have known. Never have realised the true depths of the two men who had been supposed to love her the most, but had revealed themselves to have betrayed her in the greatest of ways.

Roman stood before his foe, using the old man's silence to take in the changes in his grandfather over the last eighteen years. He searched Vladimir's face, hating the strange similarities between him and his mother. Between Vladimir and himself.

An almost dizzying sense of satisfaction roared through him as he finally held Vladimir in the palm of his hand. And the urge to squeeze, to destroy, to remove the man from the face of this earth was overwhelming. Until Vladimir laughed.

'So cocky. So arrogant. And so convinced that you have everything *you* want. But you are wrong. All these years I knew that you would want your revenge. I saw it in your eyes that day. And if you hadn't been the bastard son of my disowned daughter I might have even respected you for it, recognised you as part of my own flesh and blood.'

Roman worked hard to keep his face impassive. Unease stirred in his breast for the first time as he began to feel the steel traps close around him—but, like all prey, still vainly hoping that he was wrong.

'Did you know that your mother was to be married to Nathaniel Riding? That all I ever wanted was to secure our business partnership with an unbreakable bond of family? When instead *she* chose that carpenter it nearly destroyed the business, ruining everything that I had worked for years to achieve. Nathaniel soon got over the disappointment, but I did not. Imagine—my own daughter being my near undoing. So when I realised what a beautiful creature Ella would become, I knew that I had the perfect bait…for you. The innocent, naïve young woman who would tempt you into playing your hand. And I safeguarded that innocence. That naivety. Giving her everything she would need to be the perfect focus of your attention. All I ever wanted was the joining of the two families. Mine and the Ridings'. And you have delivered it to me on a plate.

'You want the company? It's all yours. After all, you've achieved what I could never have done. You have proved the lengths you will go to, the very depths, and that is what makes you worthy. Finally, I see myself in you. That is why you deserve it.'

The rattling cackle that left the old man's lips nearly destroyed him. Everything he'd ever wanted disappeared in a heartbeat—vengeance turned to ash on his tongue as Roman realised that all this time, all these years he'd thought himself better, quicker, smarter, and he'd done everything Vladimir had expected of him and more.

Roman felt a helpless fury ricochet through his body, every nerve, every cell vibrating with the power of it. Refusing to give the bastard the satisfaction of seeing it, Roman stalked from the room, the sound of laughter chasing at his heels.

He slammed the door behind him and turned, coming face to face with his bride. A bride who had clearly overheard every word.

Ella had stayed for one reason and one reason only. The vain hope that when she looked into her husband's eyes she would see some kind of explanation. Some kind of reason or justification for taking the threads of her life and pulling them apart. Over the course of the conversation she had put together enough meaning, enough understanding of the need for vengeance, and the horrifying game the two men had played over the years. But still—beating deep within her—was the hope that in spite of it all there was some trace of the man she had married. Yet in his eyes she saw nothing but anger and hatred, resentment and fury. Those emotions suddenly detonated within her, forging her own rage in a flame burst that threatened to consume her.

She slapped him. Hard and fast across his cheek, before stumbling half-blindly past Dorcas, who seemed torn between her master and her new mistress, past Konstantin, whose longstanding self-containment seemed sorely tested, and into the back of the limousine.

When the driver asked her where to, all she could reply was Paris. After a beat, the man put the car into gear and whisked her away, saying nothing to the command to cross several countries in the middle of the night.

As the estate grew small in the distance Ella vowed that she would never let herself be so cruelly used by these two men ever again. She would not let this destroy her. She would find a way. A way to cut them from her life, a way to secure her own freedom. And she would never, ever believe in fairy tales ever again.

CHAPTER FOUR

*It was wrong of the wolf to have underesti-
mated Little Red Riding Hood. An oversight on
his part and one that would change everything
he thought he knew.*

   The Truth About Little Red Riding Hood
                              —Roz Fayrer

IT HAD BEEN eight months since Ella had set foot in
Russia and though it felt as if everything in her life
had changed, the landscape around her hadn't. She
stood in the gardens of Vladimir's estate in Rublevka
on the outskirts of Moscow, nestled amongst the
houses of various celebrities and the Russian elite.
Snow lay thickly on the ground even this far into
March, covering the sprawling garden in a strange
white blanket, but her waterproof knee-high boots
prevented the frigid dampness from reaching her. All
the lights were on in the grand neoclassical building
behind her, casting a false warmth on the bleak horizon. But only she and one other remained. Konstan-

tin would stay on for another month, closing down Vladimir's vast and deeply secretive estate, his pension well accounted for in the terms of Kolikov's will.

Her guardian's life goal of uniting the two families locked within his once vast empire complete, Vladimir had finally succumbed to pneumonia and passed away seven days before. And she didn't know how to feel. How to feel about a man who had used her as bait, but had also protected and nurtured her, allowed her certain freedoms and withheld others. While there had been legal conversations conveyed through her and Vladimir's lawyers the moment she'd realised that her marriage had triggered her trust fund, only one phone call had actually passed between them.

She had expected explanations or apologies, but she'd been mistaken. Again. She had felt so horribly mistaken about everything. As if every single aspect of her life had been a lie. But Vladimir's assurance during that last conversation that he had protected her interests, her trust fund and her future with Kolikov Holdings hadn't been a lie. Because while he had made good on his word to hand over control and ownership of the company he and her father had set up more than thirty years ago to Roman, Vladimir had had one last card to play. He had given her ten per cent of his shares—bringing the total, inclusive of the ones she had gained upon access to her trust fund, to twenty-five, automatically making her a shareholder on the board. Automatically handing her a voice, a bargaining chip, against the man she'd once thought of as her husband.

A man who hadn't even bothered turning up to Vladimir's funeral. Throughout the entire service her body had been on fire with nervous energy, drenched in ice-cold sweat one second and ferocious heat the next, hatred and disgust turning nauseous sweeps in her stomach. For every single minute of it, her concentration had been fractured with the expectation that Roman would appear, as if summoned by a call that even he couldn't refuse. But refuse he had. And she hadn't been the only one surprised by Roman's absence.

Various business associates Ella remembered from her childhood had come, seemingly not to pay their dubious respects to a man who had ruled with an iron fist, but instead wanting to see the fabled prodigal grandson return, each wanting to know what her husband's plans were for the company.

Ever since Célia had discovered Ella sobbing over a laptop open to a search about her husband—something she'd had neither the thought nor inclination to do during their time in France—she'd determinedly avoided any and all thoughts about Roman, Vladimir and that damned business. Célia's reassurances that Ella had been both too busy and too worried about her grandmother did nothing to protect her from her own self-disgust at the shocking naivety with which she'd met and married a stranger.

A stranger who was reportedly not only uniquely ruthless in business—a fact she now well knew—but also thoroughly disreputable between the sheets. At first she had been shocked by the contrast of the almost idyllically respectful man she had married—the one who had wanted to preserve her innocence—and the notorious playboy he was proclaimed by the world's press. It was then that she realised the true extent of his deception. That he really had only wanted one thing from her. Access to Vladimir.

And somehow that had hurt so much, so acutely that it had stolen her breath and stopped her tears.

Strangely, she had found no sympathy with her former guardian. Because there too she had done her research. The man had disowned his daughter, cutting her off both financially and emotionally, for not wanting to marry Nathaniel.

Ella shivered again at the actions of two men hell-bent on destroying each other…and her in the process. And now? All she wanted was to be free. From this, from him. From the memories of her own stupidity.

And worse, the hopes and dreams that had died that day. The ones that she had not realised she'd even had before Roman had conjured them from her like a magician. A childhood yearning for the things she had lost. And then he'd taken them away—the loss as real as if they had been solid things and not just the thin veils of heartfelt fantasies. And no matter how much she might want to erase her marriage to Roman, she knew she'd never be able to erase the mark he'd left on her heart.

And once again, as if a flame had touched the detonating cord of her anger, she was furious. Furious that Roman hadn't come to the funeral today. Hadn't bothered even to respond to the lawyers she had sent after him for a simple signature on the divorce papers she had had drawn up almost the moment she had been back in Célia's little Parisian apartment. So this was how it was to be then. The hunted would become the hunter. Ella embraced her resentment and relished the thought of tracking Roman down. It was *he* who would soon know the feeling of regret. Because she was no longer the innocent he had claimed her to have been. No. Now she was a force to be reckoned with.

Roman took a conservative mouthful of ice-cold *zubrowka*, despite wanting to down the lot in one go. He knew himself well and, loath as he was to admit it, tonight—the day his grandfather went into the cold, hard ground—would be a trigger and he wanted his wits about him. He could feel it crackling in the air about him, as if a finger from the past had pressed against the back of his neck and burned an ice-cool trail down his spine.

As much as he'd wanted to see Vladimir laid to

what he hoped would be *un*rest, a greater part of him didn't want to see his wife. For somehow throughout the last eight months he had stopped viewing Ella's fiancé as some separate part of himself and embraced the person chained, legally and bodily, to her as her husband.

Because Roman was unable to forget that kiss. It was, he'd decided, the moment the disguise had evaporated. It hadn't been Ella's fiancé who had stolen that impassioned, impulsive moment. No. It had been Roman himself. He'd wanted more. He *still* wanted more. He was not such a Neanderthal that he put the constant state of his frustration down to the fact he hadn't spent time in a woman's bed for nearly ten months now. He knew he could have had his pick ever since leaving Kolikov's estate. But he hadn't. It had struck him with a painful irony that some of Ella's fiancé had rubbed off on him, and all the talk of the sanctity of marriage had somehow bled into him.

And it was that which was most threatening to him. That he had begun to believe his own lies. Begun to meld parts of the fiancé to parts of himself. In truth, it wasn't just marital faithfulness that had wrapped around his conscience, but some unfathomable desire for something beyond revenge and vengeance. Some unnerving yearning for something he'd long thought himself not only incapable of, but utterly immune to. A craving that scratched at him from the inside, rolled around his chest, one that took effort to beat back down.

In its place he sought the safer familiarity of anger, the need for revenge, but even that had been infected, ruined by the near gut-churning agony of realising that he had never really got his vengeance. Roman's deathbed promise to his mother had gone unfulfilled and he hated himself for it, whilst hating Vladimir more. But the one overriding question he couldn't help voicing to himself in the deepest, darkest nights was whether Ella had known. Whether she had been playing him too. He knew it wouldn't be answered until he looked her in the eye. Which was—as he repeatedly told himself—the only reason he had so far refused to sign the divorce papers her lawyers insisted on peppering him with.

As he took another controlled sip of his drink, in the back office of his nightclub in Moscow, Dorcas shifted by his feet. He'd not been able to rid himself of the beast. She had persistently followed him wherever he'd gone, seemingly not put out by either the noises of his clubs nor the strangely isolated life he'd returned to. And he'd come to enjoy the discomfort of the board members of Kolikov Holdings when they realised Dorcas would be attending his business meetings. It did great work in putting them on the back foot.

She had appeared to mope, somewhat disconcertingly for the first few months, roaming the rooms and halls as if looking for Ella. But she had finally settled into some long-term sulk that was appeased only by food or a good ear rub.

His mind returned to the question of Ella's involvement in his grandfather's plans. He appreciated the irony of doubting the truth of her intentions, despite the sheer villainy of his own. But with more than a few months' distance, the assurance of her innocence had begun to fade. Because surely no one raised by Vladimir Kolikov could have ever been that innocent.

As he scanned the security feeds of the club in his back office, he paused, frowned and returned to the previous screen, his fingers tightening around the small cut-glass tumbler.

Ella Riding. His salvation or damnation, for her to decide.

She looked up at the waistcoated barman, who appeared oddly like an old-world Victorian with the most improbable handlebar moustache. She'd not known what to expect from Roman's figurehead bar. Perhaps something a little more…seedy? A den of iniquity? Writhing, scantily clad women whose skin glowed beneath harsh red lighting even.

But certainly not this, with Art Deco stained glass designs across the ceiling and behind the bar, backlit and throwing soft yellows, greens and blues across a space full of dark wooden booths designed for privacy. The lighting somehow made the bar feel out of time—it could have been one in the afternoon rather than the morning, each of the customers seemingly ready to begin their night's festivities rather than coming to the end of it.

It was, she ruefully acknowledged, beautiful. She ordered a single glass of ice-cold vodka from the barman who, much to her satisfaction, couldn't seem to take his eyes off her. She had dressed purposefully for her task here. And while she would never usually wear such a thing, the skin-tight scarlet dress, slashed down almost to her waist, was having the desired effect. Because Ella had realised the need for disguise since she had married Roman Black. And now she would wield it as well as he once had.

Konstantin, still proving his complete and utter efficiency, had located Roman at this bar, at this very moment. And while Ella knew that she could ask, or even look, for her husband, another thing she had learned was that it was more important for the prey to come to the hunter. As *she* once had.

And her husband would come to her. She knew it as well as she knew her own mind. She'd done her research, and she'd planned and prepared this time. No longer would she wait to be used by others. She would be the one in control.

As she took a sip of her vodka, her eyes connected with a man openly staring at her with an invitation that needed no words. He was tall, attractive, but utterly uninteresting to her. Just as she was considering whether it would suit her purpose to appear to entertain such an invitation, the hair at her nape raised and the skin on her arms pebbled with goose bumps. She felt a bank of heat at her back, the towering presence looming over her from behind and, if that hadn't been confirmation enough, the look on the other man's face dropped as his eyes glazed over, having taken in the presence over her shoulder, and he turned away quickly.

Her pulse flickered, and she hated the fact that Roman still held this sensual power over her. But not for long. Tonight she would get him to sign the divorce papers. Tonight she would finally be free.

'I hope you didn't wear that to the funeral. Otherwise they'd have been digging at least four more graves for the board members whose heart attacks you would have ensured.'

She silently cursed, having forgotten, or chosen to ignore, the effect his dark tones once had on her. Still refusing to turn, she placed the glass on the table before her and, head held high, steeled herself.

'From what I hear, that would have done you a favour. Tell me, is all well? Or is there something rotten in the state of Kolikov Holdings?'

'Sarcasm doesn't suit you.'

'Really? I'm surprised you think you know me well enough to say so.'

'How well do I know you? That is a very good question and one I've been wondering for quite some time now.'

* * *

Roman skirted the table, refusing to stare any longer at the backless dress revealing more of his wife than he'd ever seen. The distracting need to run a thumb, or tongue, down the length of her spine had nearly embarrassed him. Not that the view from the front was any better—his hungry eyes ate up the inches of smooth pale skin between the shocking red fabric of her dress at her chest.

Forcing his eyes to her face, he saw she was both the same and somehow changed. At first, he thought the signs subtle. The way she held herself before his unwavering gaze, the way she was dressed. But perhaps this was who she had been all along and he had been taken in as much as she.

Her hair was twisted up into a knot held high at the back of her head. Not even a stray tendril spoke to the softness of her that he had once relished. The coldness in her eyes did nothing to dampen his arousal, only inflame.

Worthy.

That was what he thought. She was now worthy of doing battle with him.

'What does it matter how well you knew me? You got what you wanted.'

'We both know I didn't. Not really.'

'And that is my fault?' she demanded, just an edge of heat to her words betraying the smooth, calm, icy exterior.

He didn't react, didn't move a muscle. He felt every inch the predator he knew she believed herself to be—and he relished it. This was what he had hoped lay beneath the soft innocence she'd presented to him before. This thread of steel, encasing a molten core of passion and heat.

'You have the audacity to try to blame me?' she said on a half laugh, as if incredulous. 'You made your bed, Roman. It would seem to be beneath your dignity to whine about it.'

Her easy dismissal roused his ire. 'You come to me in that dress and talk of beds, Ella? It would be remiss of me not to warn you against such a thing.'

'Still looking out for my innocence, husband?'

Choosing not to answer her question, he pressed on. 'Did you know?'

'Know what?' She was playing with him. He could tell she understood what he wanted to know.

'What Vladimir was up to. Did you know?'

There was part of Ella—a very large part—that wanted to say yes. Wanted him at least to believe that she had been more in control in that month in France than she had been in reality. Wanted him to think she'd had the upper hand all this time. But she couldn't. She didn't want to be part of this cycle of hatred. It made her feel dirty and disgusted.

'I didn't even know what *you* were up to. How on earth was I supposed to know what my guardian was planning?' She saw his gaze narrow, searching her features, her disgust and resentment plain and clear. 'Would it make it easier for you? If I had been? Would that somehow excuse the horrifying lengths you went to achieve your revenge?'

Only because she had been studying his face as fiercely as he studied hers did she think that just this once she had struck home. That she might have been right. But she refused to credit Roman with enough conscience for that.

'Well, I didn't. Up until that night, I'd only known my guardian as the man who rescued me, gave me a home, education, security—'

'All the things he should have given his own daughter.'

'Is that why? Why you took your vengeance out on me? Because in some way you thought I had stolen what was rightfully your mother's?' She needed to know. It was the one burning question that cut through her like a knife. The fear that somehow she *was* responsible for bringing his vengeance down on her too.

'I took my revenge *through* you because, for a moment, I forgot what a cold unfeeling bastard my grandfather was and thought that he might have actually valued you as opposed to using you as bait.'

He spat the words out at her and if he regretted them, she simply couldn't tell any more.

'So, I was inconsequential to you both in your double-edged plans for vengeance.'

'Inconsequential? Do you know what it was like? To turn up at that estate, to have to beg a man for whom money was no concern for the equivalent of a measly twenty thousand euros for medical treatment that would have saved his daughter's life?'

Ella had wanted to know, had wanted to understand, but this? This was horrifying to her. Growing up, she'd been aware that Vladimir had once had a daughter and had believed the silence surrounding her had something to do with the grief he'd felt. She'd even been touched by the idea that they had been brought together by loss. Him somehow replacing her parents, and her Vladimir's lost child. And when she'd learned that he'd cut her off she'd been horrified. But to think that he'd held within his power the chance to save his own child and said no? It seemed almost impossible. Nausea mixed with the ice-cold vodka in her stomach, curdling, turning and twisting in her thoughts.

Now it was Roman's turn to exhale a bitter laugh. 'Why am I not surprised? Of course your loving guardian wouldn't have admitted that he'd had the chance to save his daughter's life and chosen not to.'

Rallying as quickly as possible, she pressed on. 'I am not responsible for the actions of a man who took those actions before I was even at school.' But guilt? Yes. She did feel guilty for all that she'd been given and all that his mother had been denied. And somewhere deep down she also felt heartbroken for the child who had been denied, the young boy she could see simmering beneath the surface of this dark façade her husband had come to wear, a boy who would have begged and pleaded for help to save his mother.

Despite her flatly delivered refusal, he could see the truth shining in her eyes. His wife was not such a great actress after all, and had clearly been as much in the dark as he about Vladimir's plans to dangle her like bait. Nor could he fail to see the open wound he had poked and prodded with the reminder of just how badly she had been used by Vladimir.

'Why are you here?' he demanded, seeking a reason to avoid the reminder that he had inflicted his own damage upon her. 'Because I doubt it was to rehash the past.' Instead he focused on words that would bring back his worthy opponent. 'You turn up on the night of my grandfather's funeral dressed like sin and my only conclusion can be that you want something—but I think it would be remiss of me to assume.'

'It would. I want a divorce.'

He'd known it was coming. Had been ignoring emails and letters sent to his office by her team of lawyers for some time now. Yet inexplicably he wanted to prolong this moment.

'And what if I suddenly find I don't want a divorce from my delicious wife?'

'Then you'd better rethink your intentions. Because I have nothing left to lose.' Her simple declaration sliced into his skin, the accusation hitting his usually impenetrable heart infallibly. 'You, however, have a great deal to lose.' He felt everything in him rear up at the warning. This wife of his should not be underestimated and suddenly he found himself enjoying this new version of her. This determined and confident woman was much more intriguing than the guileless young woman from France.

'So,' she pressed on, 'if you choose not to grant the annulment you taunted Vladimir with, then I will make myself deeply inconvenient for you.'

He scoffed. 'How do you think you could do that?'

'As someone with twenty-five per cent of the shares of Kolikov Holdings, left to me by my father's trust fund, and now by Vladimir, a number that automatically makes me a shareholding partner rather than a silent one, I think I could become quite a problem for you.'

Shock cut through him like a knife. A physical reaction that wasn't missed by his newly determined wife and, much to his chagrin, she laughed, the cool sound scraping over suddenly sensitive nerves. That bastard. His grandfather had not only fooled him, tricked him, but, further than that, he'd had the last laugh.

'You might have got the company name,' she said,

'you might have got the CEO's position, but did you think Vladimir would make it that easy? Did you think *I* would make it that easy after what you did to me? If I were of a mind I could start by renewing my friendship with the members of the board. Is Burian still trying to brew his own beer? He would always try and get Vladimir to drink the stuff. And what about Evgeni and Illarion? Are they still trying to compete with each other over who can out-gift the other at Christmastime? Such dear men and so *very* kind to me growing up.'

Roman struggled to laugh off her warning. 'I don't think you know those men as well as you think you do. Each and every one of them would sell their grandmother for a greater payout.'

'That might be the case. But this company isn't the only thing you care about, is it? After all, your reputation is one of the things that makes men quake in their boots. How do you think they would feel to see you brought low by your wife?'

'And just how do you think you might achieve such a thing?'

'As my own reputation means so very little to me, I would be more than happy to create such a scandal that you would see my face everywhere you went, every newspaper, every online article—I would make sure that the world knew that the Great Wolf's wife was bringing him to his knees.'

She was joking. Surely.

'Imagine—the wife of the world's greatest seducer looking elsewhere for her pleasure. What would that do to your precious reputation?'

'You're an innocent, you wouldn't even know how,' he declared.

He watched in horrified fascination as his wife turned her gaze from his to some poor dolt at the neighbouring table. Roman hadn't spared a glance at him, but the other man had obviously not done the same for Ella—who now focused her entire being on him. A quirked eyebrow and delicious curve of red-painted lips brought a blush to the man's cheeks. Before he took in Roman's scowling features, put his drink down and made his way to a safe distance on the other side of the room.

Ella turned back to Roman, the look in her eyes unadulterated victory.

'My virtue is meaningless, my innocence destroyed. You saw to that. You like to think that you're the big bad wolf, but I was raised by the biggest, baddest wolf of them all. You taught me revenge and vengeance and I might just find that I enjoy it.'

CHAPTER FIVE

And the wolf smiled. For Red Riding Hood had
knocked upon the door and in a heartbeat he
would bid her enter. And once he had her where
he wanted her...there would be no turning back.
       The Truth About Little Red Riding Hood
                              —Roz Fayrer

SOMETHING INFERNAL ROARED within him. Hot, hard
and angry. He was angry that she would try to seduce
another in front of him, and also angry on her behalf.
She had no idea what kind of power she wielded. Es-
pecially looking like that. He hadn't lied when he'd
said she looked like sin. All the images crashing
through his mind taunted him with what he could not
have. Writhing in his mind as if on silk bed sheets.

The sheer naivety of trying to get at him, at his
reputation by sleeping with another man, infuriated
him. Not that for one moment he believed that she'd
actually go through with it. But Ella's fiancé had
fought hard with Roman not to give in to his baser

desires and take her time and time again in France. All those opportunities he'd turned back from in order not to ruin her innocence and here she was, just wanting to throw it away?

He rounded the table, grasped her elbow and practically dragged her through the bar towards the bank of discreet lifts at the back.

'That wasn't seduction, that was an open invitation.'

'Where are we going?'

'Somewhere private to have this conversation. A place where the patrons of my establishment won't be subjected to a crude opening of the bedroom door which would have left you both unsatisfied and grieving for the loss of your innocence.'

With the swipe of his key card the lift doors opened and, despite the urge to practically throw her into the small space, he released her elbow and gestured for her to enter before him.

She did so, surprisingly without argument, and he stepped in to face her. 'Seduction is about power,' he said, looming over her, yet also trying desperately not to make physical contact, not to touch a millimetre of the deliciously small form practically vibrating with the same ferocious energy he felt building within him. 'The giving and taking of it, subtly shifting between the seducer and the seduced. I do not think you are ready for that.'

'I am not the girl I once was,' she said. He gave

her credit for managing to keep the tremors of her body from her voice.

'And I am not the man you married.'

'So, who are you then?' she demanded.

'The man who is trying to show you that, should you choose to go down that path, you would only get yourself into more trouble than you are in now.'

The lift arrived and the doors parted to reveal his penthouse apartment. But Ella saw none of the incredible views of Moscow from the expansive floor-to-ceiling windows that took up the entire length and width of the side wall. She saw nothing of the expensively decorated room, the fireplace and sprawling leather sofa that could have easily seated six people. Instead, the sheer dismissal of Roman's reaction to her threat had fired outrage within her breast. An outrage that contained a hint of the hurt that her husband had refused to touch her, that the Great Wolf, as the newspapers had reported him to be, the *'errant seducer',* had chosen to leave her innocent.

And that wall of heat, that fire within her wanted it all to burn. Every last shred of a connection between her and this man.

'Oh, how very kind of you to look after my innocence now. After you took everything I knew and tore it down.'

'Everything you knew? Really? You met and married a man within five weeks. I did not force you into it.'

His words taunted her, scratched at wounds not yet healed. 'You lied to me.'

'It was a kindness. I didn't have the luxury of lies growing up.'

'A kindness?'

'Yes. Would you rather I'd kidnapped you and forced you?'

She wanted to growl, to scream her rage. 'You present two equally awful options and ask me which is better?'

'I did not blackmail you, nor abuse your body. Your innocence is no defence against your own actions, and ignorance is no excuse.'

'Who are you trying to convince? Me or yourself?' she demanded.

'Don't you think it is better to know the truth about Vladimir? He used you as bait for me. Does that not outrage you?'

'You think it worse to be used by him than you?'

'Yes. Trust in that. If not me, then there would have been worse options out there.'

'You think there is worse out there than what you did to me?' Ella said, unable to wrap her head around the fact that her husband clearly thought himself a saviour of sorts.

'Yes. Believe it or not, there are. Ones who wouldn't have stopped themselves from taking everything you had on offer, including your innocence and much more.'

'Don't you dare paint yourself in some heroic light, rescuing me from a fate worse than you.'

'I didn't come after your money or your body.'

'I hate you,' she growled, finally letting loose all the pent-up energy and hurt accrued over the last eight months.

'Good. Now you might just understand a fraction of what I felt for my grandfather.'

Roman turned away in frustration, stalking towards the window and passing a hand through his hair rather than reaching for her and shaking her as he wanted to do—shake some sense into the woman his wife had become. But he hadn't brought her to his apartment to talk about the past. No. Now he was working towards damage limitation for her and himself. He had to persuade her from her ridiculous plan. Had to show her the dangerous fire she was playing with.

Spinning back to her, he pressed on. 'Tell me. What would you do once you found the unsuspecting key to your revenge against me, Ella? Would you be able to do what I did? Would you be able to seduce? To bend another to your will?'

He snared her with his gaze and took slow deliberate steps towards her, the unconsciously lithe movements catching her attention and widening her eyes.

'Because true seduction involves the chase.' This he could do. This he could give her. A final lesson to teach her the error of her plans. 'It's about timing. When to make your move. Not when you are ready, but when *they* are.'

As if conjuring the very thing he wanted to warn her against, he watched as her body turned to him, in tune with his every movement, and cursed both her and himself to hell and damnation.

'It is the appreciation of what your prey is feeling,' he said as her eyes flared as much as his own arousal, no longer able to ignore the way that his body had reacted to hers. The way her nipples had pebbled beneath the tight confines of her dress, the way her breath hitched, caught in her throat, as if equally under the sensual spell he was weaving between them.

'The heady sense of anticipation when they know what's coming and no longer fight it but actively want it. When every nerve, every cell of their body is on fire with need, with desire, an intensity that becomes almost undeniable. It's the moment when your prey is most alive, ready and willing to succumb to their own desire.'

He was bare inches from her now, no longer sure who was the seducer or the seduced, his breath just as ragged as her own.

'You talk of seduction and power as if you didn't already know that you had all the power all along?' Ella threw at the man mere inches from her, crowding her in the most delicious of ways. She hated what her body wanted, the yearning that almost choked her. The need. Her only defence ineptly thrown barbs at a man who seemed more well versed in the cravings of her own body than herself.

'Really? And what if I gave you all the power now? What would you take from me? How would you exact your revenge? Is it a signature you want or is there something else?'

Her mind stopped. Short-circuited. Instead, it threw up images of her deepest, darkest dreams from the last eight months. Fantasies of a wedding night that had never been, ones that she could barely admit to herself even though she'd woken up morning after morning hot and exhausted, aching with an unsatisfied need. A need that only one man could truly satisfy.

'Is that why you're really here? Do you know as much as I that we have unfinished business?' he demanded, his words surprisingly soft, gentle almost, seductive.

'Says the man who reportedly *saved* my innocence,' she bit out angrily.

He leaned into her then, closing the small space between them, dipping his head to whisper in her ear. 'Says the woman who would give it away to have her revenge.'

He pulled back, his eyes raking over her body as if looking for something, some kind of sign—something she feared that her body would betray. Had perhaps already betrayed.

'What if I said that you could take your vengeance out on *me*? Right here, right now?' Once again, her husband was pulling the rug from beneath her. Turning her words and intentions against her. Because suddenly she wanted that more than anything. She barely had the time to wonder if she had been fooling herself all along. If she had, in fact, come here with that one purpose.

'What if I gave you one night—*just this night*—to take whatever it is you want? Because, Ella, I would lay myself prostrate on that funeral pyre and die a happy man.'

The raw admittance, guttural and dark with desire, completely undid her. A strange heady sense of vulnerability, the image of her husband willingly giving her whatever she desired for this one night, fired a heat deep within her until she ached, a sob of need rising within her chest threatening to escape.

'And I am supposed to believe a word that comes out of your mouth?' Her last line of defence, half begging and half pleading, for what outcome, she no longer knew.

'Then don't believe my words… Believe this.'

His lips claimed hers with an almost primal need. These were not the same gentle sweet-tasting lies pressed against her lips she remembered. This was raw, unadulterated desire. Seeking, demanding, expecting.

She gasped as her mouth opened to his, desperately seeking oxygen that only served to feed the fire within her. The fire of need and want and so much more. Yes, she admitted to herself, this was what she had wanted.

Ever since she had first seen him, Ella had sensed this about him, had desired and coveted it. All her imaginings of how she would feel, what it would be like, paled in comparison as his arms swept around her, his hands trailing fire across her body, over her breasts and clutching at her hips, drawing her into him, against him, against his arousal. Showing her his own need for her.

'This is what you do to me, Ella. Does that please you?'

Ella could not speak, could barely think to respond, but her body knew. She groaned into his kiss, the shocking sound of her own desire undeniable. Her hands flew to his chest, her mind warring with her heart as she fisted the cotton of his shirt, claiming and owning her own need for him in a way that shocked her.

While his tongue plundered her mouth, rendering her senseless to anything but the raw passion he was building within her, his hands teased up the taut hemline of her skirt a few inches, his fingers reaching beneath to mould her thighs and backside with his palms. Her passionate cries were nothing compared to the growl of raw want that vibrated across her skin.

Drawing back, he spun her in his arms and pressed her against the wall of the room, her arms coming up to brace against the strangely soothing cool panel. His body leaned against her from behind and he pressed open-mouthed kisses to her neck, nudging her head to one side to give himself better access to the sensitive area behind her ear. Held like this, she felt completely surrounded, crowded but deliciously so, desperate for more, for something she couldn't quite explain.

His hand clutched the nape of her neck briefly, strongly, a display of his power, there and gone in a moment, as he pressed the pad of his thumb to the top of her spine and traced the outline to where the material of her dress barely covered the curve of her hips. She arched into the touch, pressing her breast into his other hand, and nearly cried out as he ran a knuckle over her hardened nipple.

His hands covered her, worshipped her, slipping beneath the material that barely covered her breast and causing her to lean back against him, against the hard ridge of his arousal. Her head drew back to rest against his shoulder, her breathing harsh and her cries of pleasure falling about them, discarded in the air.

'So glorious. So magnificent...' Roman's words

were a continuation of the seduction his body was performing.

His hand swept around her neck, cupping her chin in his palm, and she couldn't help but bend into it, taking his finger into her mouth where his tongue had been, sucking on him, consuming him in any way she could.

She felt him tremble behind her, the action sending fierce satisfaction through her to have this man as weak with need as she was. And then he turned her in his arms once again, to face him, a raised eyebrow taking in that power she felt, appreciating her own power, encouraging it even. The harsh slash of red across his cheeks speaking of his arousal, the ferocity of his gaze speaking of his need.

'Will you let me give you this, Ella? For just this one night?'

She knew what he was asking. That, no matter how much of a villain she had painted him in her mind, he would not give what she would not willingly take.

And she did want to take it. She wanted to take him. All of him.

'This will be the end of your thoughts and plans of revenge. I will grant you the divorce you wish for.'

Something deep within her rent apart. She knew, with more certainty than she had ever thought he'd loved her, that this was not a condition but a gift of sorts upon parting. It was this that would symbolise the removal of Roman from her life. Not a signature on a piece of paper, but one indelibly written on her body.

'Yes.'

As if the leash had been loosened on the last threads of his restraint, Roman claimed her once again. His lips crashed against hers, his tongue, glorying in its freedom, pressed into the warm wet heat of her mouth.

If he'd known what she would be like beneath his touch, his kiss, he would not have been able to leave her untouched previously. Every inch of him was drenched with a need he'd never before experienced. He sought not to disguise the way his body trembled but to relish it as he realised that it fed her own desire, her own want. He had not lied when he'd promised to prostrate himself before her. Nor had he lied when he'd proclaimed he'd die a happy man.

His hands went to where his fingers had tripped over the zip as he'd caressed her body, pulling at the tab at the side of the dress and sliding it downward.

She stood before his gaze, unwavering. Only the pulse beating erratically at her throat, her cornflower-blue eyes almost black with desire, the flush across her cheeks speaking of how desperately she was clinging to her own control. And, bastard that he was, he wanted it gone, he wanted her completely at the mercy of her own desire. For if this was to be it, if this was to be their one and only night together before he signed the divorce papers severing their connection, he would give her everything she'd ever wanted in the way that her fiancé had never been able to.

'Take it off,' he commanded.

He saw the flash of defiance spark in her eyes, saw her internal war as she battled with his demand, battled with what she wanted and what she thought she should want.

He hadn't lied when he'd told her that seduction was the giving and taking of power. And if Ella had even an ounce of an idea of how much power she wielded in that moment she would have used it to destroy him completely.

Her hands swept up to the straps on her shoulders and brushed aside the scarlet material. His gaze locked on to the acres of smooth pale skin it revealed as it fell from her body and she kicked it aside with feet still encased in the highest of red leather heels. Her perfect breasts were bare to him, nipples taut and deliciously teasing, as she breathed in deeply beneath his gaze. Her narrow waist flared at her hips, where the smallest of thongs remained to hide the last vestiges of her modesty.

Red. He would always see her in red. And suddenly the memory of the red cape he had bought to replace the one damaged on their first meeting flashed into his mind. But now was not the time for thoughts or fantasies of the past. Now was the time for taking.

He stalked towards her in one powerful stride and halted the moment she placed a hand between them, stopping him in his tracks.

'Now you,' she commanded with the power he thought she did not realise she could wield.

He inhaled quickly, sharply, impossibly aroused by her self-possession.

His hands went to the tie around his neck and levered it free, pulling at the silk and casting it aside carelessly. The more she watched, the more her gaze consumed his actions, the more want and desire raged within him. Slowly and deliberately he freed the buttons of his shirt one by one, pulling the cotton from his chest and toeing off his shoes.

When his hands grasped the buckle of his belt, he almost halted his actions, torturously delaying the moment, testing the limits of his self-control. For, no matter how self-possessed Ella appeared to be, he could not forget that she was innocent. That this would be her first time. But he would make sure that this night would be everything he could never give her in the cold light of day. Or any day from here on in. Because this was the last time he would see his wife.

A wife who, for all his protestations, he *had* manipulated, *had* coerced into doing his bidding. Well, now he would willingly do hers.

He drew aside the leather belt with a snap, slipping it through the loops holding it in place and tossing it aside. As he drew down the fastenings of his trousers, Ella turned away, once again halting his progress in an instant.

'If you have changed your mind—?'

'No,' she said, bringing her gaze back to his.

'Then see. See what you do to me,' he demanded as he removed his trousers and boxers in one sweep and stood before her, more naked even than she. Bearing every caress of her gaze, proud and powerful beneath it. 'I am yours to do with as you wish,' he said. 'You wanted your revenge, you wanted the loss of the innocence you claim to no longer have. You threatened to take some unworthy other. But I am here. The heart of your vengeance and most definitely worthy of it. So take me.'

As if he had given her permission to feel, to want, to have…she closed the distance between them and claimed his lips with hers. To be on the receiving end of such a kiss nearly undid him. Instead of wrapping her arms around him as he had expected, her hands went to his thighs, her nails digging in deliciously to the hardened corded muscle before they swept around to his backside, moulding, pressing, gripping and he allowed her to feast on him.

His hands reached for her hips, pulling her against him, the skin to skin full body contact stoking an already out of control fire between them. But while she took her pleasure from him, he wanted more. To give more. Picking her up, he marvelled at the slight weight of her in his arms. As she wrapped her legs around his waist, he maintained the kiss as he walked them through his apartment to the bedroom beyond.

With one arm still wrapped around her, holding her to him, he gently laid her back across his bed and took just one moment to capture the image, burying it deep within him, knowing that, as much as he might deny it, he would remember it for the rest of his life.

Pressing a trail of open-mouthed kisses from her neck to her navel, his hands traced down her sides and beneath her to her hips.

'Do you trust me?' he asked.

Her eyes locked with his. 'No.'

An ice-cold shard cut through him, deep.

'Do you trust me in *this*?' he roughly bit out, knowing that he would stop if he needed to, but battling and raging against it.

'Yes.'

'Turn over.'

As he smoothed a hand down the length of her spine, Ella practically curved into his touch, still unable to account for why having him pressed against her back made her feel safe, made her feel secure.

She hadn't lied to him. She might not trust him with her heart, but she did trust him with her body.

She felt kisses against her shoulders, a tongue against her skin sending shooting sparks to her nipples and between her legs. Her hands gripped the cotton sheets beside her and she wanted to both curl and unfurl into them at the same time. To protect herself against the onslaught of need he was creating and open herself up to it, to take it in, to relish nothing more than the passion that was burning between them. Her whole body ached with the desire for something intangible to her, throbbing and building, both wanting and fearing the dizzying incomprehensible need within her.

He gently pulled at her hips, her body moving, lifting to where he wanted her. She felt his hands part her legs slightly as she levered herself up on her hands and cried out in both shock and pleasure when she felt his tongue at her core.

The growl of his own pleasure made her wanton as he sucked on her, his tongue delving into her from behind, her heart almost stopping from sheer ecstasy. Her arms began to shake with need, her body overriding any sense or sensibility, pressing gently back against his mouth and when she would pull away his hand at her hip held her fast, refusing her the ability to hide from this, refusing to halt the insurmountable pleasure beating harder than her heart in her chest.

His hand stretched out across her body to grasp her own where it gripped the cotton sheets, the feel of his fingers intertwining with hers a touch that moved her deeply. An assurance that she had not known she needed.

He whispered in her ear, telling her in Russian that it was okay, that she could let go. But she didn't know what she should let go of, clinging instead to the precipice of some unfathomable, undefinable point. The hand at her hip released her and she felt his knuckle against the soft throbbing core, wringing even more pleasure from her. But when she felt his finger thrust into her she fell, blindly and willingly, over the edge, while his arms held her, turning her onto her back, enfolding her so that she never hit the floor.

Watching Ella come apart in his hands had been almost indescribable. Almost, because Roman couldn't halt the words taunting his mind—words like incredible, unimaginable, impossible—or the feeling of awe within his chest. But, more terrifying, was a feeling of humility—something he could afford to neither voice nor consider.

As Ella ran a shaking hand down the arm that held her, and further towards his hip and groin, his body flared beneath her touch, reigniting an almost painful want within him. But tonight wasn't about him—it was about her.

'What do you need?' he asked her.

'You.'

That simple declaration unfurled something infernal within him, a need of his own that he'd never before experienced. He reached to the bedside table and retrieved a condom, feeling her gaze scrape against his bare skin as he tore the foil casing. The weight of her eyes on him furthered his arousal as he rolled the latex over his length.

Her body, still damp from exertion, shifted beneath him, her legs unconsciously widening to make room for him. Only the slight hesitation in her eyes gave him pause.

'Will it hurt?'

Not as much as the vulnerability in your eyes hurts me now, he thought.

'Perhaps a little. For a moment. But I will do everything in my power to lessen it.'

She nodded, the uncertainty replaced with conviction and determination as desire overrode her concern. He picked up her hand, placing a kiss in the palm, a gesture he had never before given another woman. The smile on her lips cut him to the quick as her hand reached for his shoulder and drew him towards her with a kiss full of the trust she had offered him only for her body.

A kiss that quickly morphed into one of passion and need. Roman settled between her legs and gently, slowly entered her. He felt her muscles surround him, caught the hitch in her breath and stopped as she acclimatised to the feel of him within her. A slow exhale, slightly stuttered, burned him. He hated that he was causing her physical pain, piling it onto the emotional damage he knew he had caused.

All the hours of this evening he had seen her as worthy, never once really understanding that it was he who was not. Not worthy of the gift of her innocence, of her body. He braced his arms, looking down at her, watching as she began to settle into the feeling of him. Locking his gaze with hers, he saw nothing but wonder, awe—all open to him, offered to him. And, bastard that he was, he wanted to take it all.

He pressed further within her and she gasped, a pleasure-drenched sound that caught at his heart. Holding himself there, glorying in the feel of her around him, joined with her in a way he'd never imagined, he strained against the leash of his control. Even without moving he could sense her arousal beginning, reaching, spreading through her body into his. Her sighs turned into moans of pleasure, and still he had not moved. Feeling her body tighten around him, his own arousal teased and taunted by hers, was an indescribable pleasure he'd never before tasted. Beneath his stillness, Ella began to shift gently against him, drawing him into her own passion, seducing him towards his own orgasm, closer and closer, and still he had not moved.

Her moans became gentle cries, words no longer possible, simply the sounds of need and want passing between them. He held himself still as inexplicably he felt the roll of her orgasm build, enticing his own, both fearing and wanting the moment it would end.

His last thought, before everything came crashing down upon them, was that he had not moved. That they had both come together in a moment of stillness that changed everything.

The sound of the shower roused Ella back to consciousness. Sunlight streamed in from the uncovered windows, warming her skin in a way that felt inadequate to how she had felt throughout the night as time and time again they had reached for each other, losing themselves in a wanton sensual dream. A dream that she did not want to wake from. A dream that her body clearly hadn't as it throbbed with want and need anew.

She turned onto her back, relishing the stretch of muscles, the gentle ache from where Roman had been between her thighs. As she reached for the covers, seeking the soothing caress of the cotton against her heated skin, she took in the sight of his room—the windows, the long bank of cupboards on the opposite wall, the side table. And her heart stopped.

The envelope she had brought with her the night before, the one that had been nestled within her handbag, now lay on the side table, the paperwork levered open, a yellow tab pointing alarmingly to the space where no signature had previously been, but now was.

The sight of the divorce papers nearly robbed her of breath. And suddenly she needed to leave. Needed to get her things and go. Wanted to hide, not only from the papers but from what had happened last night. She hated the feeling that coursed over her skin, leaving goose bumps in its wake. She hated that she felt the need to hide…again. Roman had been right. She had set out to get her revenge and only given him his.

CHAPTER SIX

*If there had been a moment when the wolf could
have turned back, could have changed his mind
and left Little Red Riding Hood to her own de-
vices, it was long since gone. He'd had a taste
of her now. There was no going back.*
        The Truth About Little Red Riding Hood
                                    —Roz Fayrer

ROMAN HAD HEARD nothing from Ella for three
months since he'd emerged from the shower, breath
locked tight in his lungs, knowing that she had left·
his bed, his apartment. His life.

He'd made himself retrieve the papers from where
he'd seen them in her handbag. He'd signed them
even as his hand had shaken from the most powerful encounter he'd ever shared with a woman. Signed
them as he'd promised he would. But perhaps that
was why. Ella wasn't just any woman but his wife.
Apparently she hadn't been the only one to succumb

to the fantasy he'd woven about them on his path for revenge.

At least that was what he'd told himself that morning—that his unacknowledged hesitancy at the time had been down to sensual shock. But in the days and months since then, that moment had intruded on his thoughts. It was the pause—most likely imperceptible if anyone had been looking on—that taunted him. A heartbeat of a moment in which he'd seen a future, a whole lifetime of possibilities…

But each and every one of those possibilities required something from him that he was unable and unwilling to give. It had been a dangerous moment—poised on a precipice of temptation and damnation.

But he'd known then, and he knew now, that such a thing was impossible. Laughable even. As if he were or could ever be something other than what he was. The Great Wolf. The Lone Wolf.

And the sheer fact that it'd even given him pause was enough to put pen to paper, to punctuate his signature with a full stop that nearly broke through the page. But he could not deny that he'd begun to avoid his apartment. Avoid the memories of that one night as they gripped him from beyond the past into the present. A possessiveness he couldn't shake had taken hold and every day he searched for the signed divorce papers in his mail, every day he looked for emails from her lawyers that he'd previously ignored—anything to sever a connection he feared he might never achieve—but none came.

Dorcas had resumed her sulk, seemingly betrayed by the scent of her mistress but the absence of her presence, and happily heaped the blame at his feet. Perhaps Dorcas would have been better off with Ella. It was a thought he couldn't quite shake.

Nor could he seem to shake the almost constant state of arousal he was in. One night with his wife had not been enough to satiate the ragged beast within him, the one that prowled the edges of his mind as he had prowled the corners of his apartment in Moscow.

For three months since that night in Moscow, he'd barely been able to focus, to concentrate on what needed to be done for both his own business and the dismantling of Vladimir's. And it was three months too long as far as Roman was concerned. Which was why he was now standing outside an unassuming apartment block in Paris. Because, more than anything, he wanted to draw a line under it all.

His fist pounded on the door, perhaps a little too harshly, but he refused to keep himself in check. Instead, he relished the fury coursing through his veins. The fury that was directed solely at himself. He never should have allowed it to happen. He never would have, but she had turned up at his business, at his home, and he'd signed his own fate the moment he said, *'So take me.'*

The woman who answered the door might look like Ella but she was a completely different vision from the woman he'd last seen in his bed. She looked terrible, neither the woman he had married nor the woman he had slept with visible in the figure who stood before him, turning a horrible shade of pale.

'Are you—?'

Before he could get the sentence out of his mouth she rushed off, and Roman reeled at the sounds of her being sick in a bathroom he couldn't see.

He cursed and entered the apartment, expecting to see signs of a spectacular night out, but there were no empty bottles of wine, no signs of debauchery, only several varieties of herbal tea and what looked to be a raft of vitamins half opened on the counter.

Frowning, he took in the small, homely apartment, so different from the wide expanses of his own. Small feminine touches marked the huge difference between Ella's lifestyle and his own lone wolfish nature. His eyes pounced on the manila envelope, one he recognised from the morning of their last meeting. Had she signed them? Were there now two signatures on the paperwork?

Dorcas swept around him, pawing at the door which he presumed Ella had hidden herself behind. Ignoring the half whining dog, he turned back to the sound of the boiling kettle clicking itself off. Oddly tempted by the thought of pouring the hot water into the waiting cup, his eyes snagged on one of the many vitamin bottles and stopped.

Everything stopped.

His heart crashed in his chest as he grasped the bottle in his hand and drew it close for further inspection, for further confirmation he no longer needed. Pregnancy vitamins. White knuckles framed the name on the bottle. Ella Riding. And in that moment, he knew. He knew from the look in her eyes when she'd seen him standing at the door, before fleeing. He knew instantly that it was his. A baby. *Their* baby.

Ella took giant gulps of air from where she sat with her back against the bathroom door, her heart unaccountably in tune with the gentle whines from Dorcas scratching at the wood. She didn't even know how Roman had found her. She had been sharing the apartment with Célia for almost a year. Her name wasn't on the lease, but she didn't imagine that it would have taken much for Roman to uncover the relevant piece of information if he'd chosen to do so.

She'd thought she might have had more time. More time to figure out what to do, to figure out what it meant to her now that she was pregnant. Now that she couldn't have the divorce she'd wanted, that she couldn't have her freedom.

Because the moment she'd seen the little blue cross appear on the pregnancy test she'd known that she wouldn't, couldn't, keep Roman from her life, from their child's life. Not after what they had each experienced in their own childhoods. But that hadn't meant that she'd been able to reach out to him, to tell him about it. No. She admitted to herself now that she'd been a coward. And that just as surely as she'd taunted Roman about making his own bed, she would now have to lie in one of her own making.

Though she did not presume to know what Roman's reaction might be, she knew her own. She'd promised herself that she'd never be beholden to another's whims again and she'd meant it. But she also wanted to ensure that her child had the best chance in life for a happiness neither of its parents had so far achieved. She would do everything in her power to make sure that this child never felt an ounce of what she or Roman had. The cycle of vengeance had to end. And she could only hope that he would want that too.

Levering herself off the floor, she turned the handle on the door, only to find it immediately pressed inward by Dorcas's wet grey nose nudging the wood aside. She buried her head into Ella's hip and hand, her tail thrashing against the doorframe.

The small gesture of affection—the kind of physical comfort she hadn't known she'd needed—brought tears to her eyes but she wiped them away, knowing that she would need all her armour for the conversation that was to come.

She rounded the corner of the small living space of the apartment and stopped under the weight of Roman's intense gaze.

'Were you going to tell me?' he demanded.

'Yes.'

'When?'

She bit back a sigh, knowing that he had every right to ask such questions of her. 'If you look in the drawer to the left of the stove, you'll find a plane ticket to Russia booked for five days' time.'

'When did you find out?' His clipped words lashed at her, and she took every single one with her head held high.

'I guess about a month ago, but I wanted to make sure before I spoke to you.'

Roman looked towards the drawer she had indicated, but made no move to check the truth of her words. That he didn't touched her. Soothed her a little, fanning the dull flame of hope in her chest.

He poured the water from the kettle into the cup of tea she'd had waiting before he'd knocked on her door, before she had been ready for him, and set it on the counter top between them as if unwilling, yet, to risk any physical contact between them.

'Are you okay?' he asked finally, his focus laser-sharp as she nodded.

'Have you seen a doctor?'

She sighed her *yes* more than said it.

He nodded once. 'You will return to my side,' he

declared, inflaming the rage banked momentarily by their previous detente.

'Why?' she asked, genuinely curious.

'Does everything have to have a damn explanation?'

'Yes. In this case it does,' she replied, choosing to ignore the angry outburst. 'Because, really? There's very little between us aside from resentment and lies. And that is not something that I will inflict on my child.'

'So, you are keeping it?'

'Of course!' Ella's outraged declaration thrummed through the air between them, beating at him accusingly. 'You would ask me—?'

'No!' He couldn't even let her finish that sentence. The words, the thought that she would think him capable of such a thing, truly shocked him.

'Don't act all outraged. The lengths to which you have gone to get what you want are well documented by this point, don't you think?'

'Is that why you waited this long to tell me?' He had turned away despite his probing question, unable and unwilling to see the look on her face, to read the truth in her eyes.

'No. I waited this long to make sure my baby was safe.'

He heaved out a weighted breath which was half relief and half frustration. 'Our.'

'Our what?'

'Our baby, dammit.'

* * *

Roman cursed, already feeling a step behind, already feeling cut from his own child's life by her simple declaration, and it scalded him from the inside out. A child, the presence, the reality of which he simply couldn't wrap his head around. His hand flew to his hair, sweeping it back from his forehead, only just resisting the urge to grasp it in a fist and display his frustration for the quick gaze of his wife, consuming his reaction to this sudden news as if it were a test. One that he really feared he might fail.

He had never wanted children. Couldn't even fathom how it had happened because he knew they had used protection each and every time. But he also knew that protection failed, plans failed, and that nothing in Ella would have willingly bound herself to a monster such as him. And now he had somehow tied an irrefutable bond between him, her and... their child. An innocent child brought into his world, a world formed only from anger, vengeance, hurt.

He was going to be a father.

'What are you planning?' he asked, focusing his confusion on her rather than himself and the thoughts their child had conjured.

She sighed, delaying her response by taking a sip of the tea she cradled carefully within her hands. Refusing to let her hide from him, he stared her down, taking in all the emotions passing across her face. Emotions that echoed within him.

'I honestly don't know. I have a barely-off-the-ground business, half-signed divorce papers, no home of my own and a baby on the way.' As if by listing her current predicament had somehow brought it all to bear down upon her shoulders, she swayed a little where she stood and he cursed. He reached for her then, stopping a few inches from actually touching her and guided her towards the small sofa and chair set of the open-plan living area.

The moment she sat down Dorcas resumed her guard of his wife, placing her large head in Ella's lap and staring between them, adoringly and accusingly, depending on the focus of her gaze. He didn't have to see where Dorcas placed the blame. He felt it down to his toes.

'You are pregnant and will return to me,' he asserted, as if it were that simple. As if that would somehow make sense of everything that was swirling through his mind and heart.

'What will you threaten me with this time?' she asked, her words at odds with the almost numbness of her tone.

'I've never once threatened you. And you can say that I coerced you into marriage, but I sure as hell did not coerce you into bed.' The lack of emotion behind her words somehow ignited his own.

'No,' she agreed. 'I would never say that.' The pretty blush on any other woman could have been considered coquettish, but in Ella he knew it to be real. As real as the baby that they were to have. That she could still prevent him from having access to. And though Roman might never have wanted even the abstract idea of a child—now that Ella was carrying his heir, his flesh and blood joined with hers, it was as if something primal, something raw and ancient had gripped his heart and made him more sure of this one thing than he'd ever been in his life. That he needed his wife and child with him. So, he would do, say whatever it was that Ella needed him to say in order to secure that.

'You lost your parents at a young age. And I do not for one moment dismiss the tragedy of that,' he insisted vehemently. 'But my...*father* chose to take money instead of staying with my mother. He left her pregnant and alone. Knowing this, knowing that he chose her father over her and her child, it devastated my mother.'

Through his words, Ella heard and felt the echoes of pain that such a thing would have, in fact *had*, inflicted on Roman as a child. A pain that still held such a grip he had distanced himself from the effect of his father's actions.

'And you?'

'Any finer feelings on the matter I have long since dealt with.'

'Please don't. Please don't fob me off. I need to

understand, to know what raising our child together means to you,' she begged.

He exhaled harshly through thin lips, as if desperately fighting his own self-preservation instincts against giving her what she wanted. She could tell that this was a vulnerability that he didn't reveal to many, if at all. But, from the look in his eyes, she sensed that he understood her need to know.

'I grew up as the illegitimate son of a single mother. And, yes, there are many, many others who grow up exactly the same way. But it was different for my mother. She lost too much, sacrificed too much for me...' He trailed off, shaking his head. 'She blamed herself,' he continued through gritted teeth. '*I* blamed myself, until I was old enough to understand the selfishness of my father's actions. Growing up, my mother did everything she could to make sure that I was loved enough. She worked three jobs to keep a roof over our heads, to keep food in the fridge, and it was just us against the world. So when she got ill...'

'It was just you,' Ella concluded for him. And in that moment she realised why Roman had been so good at helping her with her grandmother. Why he had known and seemed to understand what she needed even before she'd realised it for herself. 'And you were thirteen?' she asked, pulling other details from their time together in France, adding it to what she knew had happened after Roman had gone to see

Vladimir, and her heart ached for him. Ached not only for his loss and the cruel actions of his grandfather, but for what it had caused him to become, how it had forged the path his life had taken.

'I was eleven when my mother first became ill. Tatiana had always been small, which was why she'd been such a wonderful dancer. Small but powerful,' he added with a sad smile Ella was sure was purely unconscious.

'What kind of dancer?' Ella asked the man lost to memories of his childhood.

'Ballet. Before she met my father and Vladimir disowned her, Tatiana was the principal ballerina at the Utonchennyy Ballet Company.'

Ella's shock must have shown on her face because Roman looked up and smiled, proud of his mother's incredible achievement. A pride that was both contagious and shocking. Shocking because, for just a moment, she caught a glimpse of the fiancé who had courted her, who had—at the time—appeared proud of *her*.

'But after Vladimir and her lover abandoned her she was alone, Ella. She had no one and no help. She worked herself to the bone and it didn't seem to matter how much she did, or how much she tried to love me, she never felt it was enough.

'So hear me now, Ella. My child will know me. They will bear my name and they will want for nothing in this world. They will never have to beg for anything, from *either* parent.'

That vehemence in his tone she understood. The need to protect she felt beat strongly within her own heart. Her own loss, melding with his, made her determined to find a way for them both through this. But she'd meant what she'd said when she'd proclaimed herself no longer naïve. And that forced the next words to her lips.

'I have some conditions.' He caught her gaze and gestured for her to proceed. 'I need to know who you are. I married out of deceit—I will not continue that way. Neither will I blindly sign my life and my child's life away to a man who has broken every single piece of trust I had. You cannot lie to me again.'

He nodded.

'I mean it, Roman. I will not live like that.'

'I understand.'

'And I also need to know that you are done with your plans of revenge. Which means that I need to know that you're not taking down the company.' She wavered on the edge of a precipice, half hoping and half fearing that he would agree. But she needed him to understand. 'That company might have been Vladimir's, but it was just as much my father's. It is a part of our child's history.'

'A history that you would own? How on earth do you plan to explain that to our child?' he demanded, anger vibrating within his words. 'That company was more important to Vladimir than his own daughter and even you. How can you want anything to do with it?'

Everything he'd ever done, every single achievement, every single motivation, goal and broken thing within him, had been about bringing the destruction of Vladimir's company and now she wanted him to keep it? His heart rent in two, half denying her request and half ready to do whatever she wanted.

'It is the only thing I have left of my father. A father I barely remember. And, like you, that is not something I want my child to experience. So I would very much like you to agree to my conditions. But know this—if, at the end of the next five months I don't want to be in a relationship with you, then you will buy my shares from me, give me a divorce and let me go.'

'Why would I buy your shares?'

'Because if I don't want to be married to you, then I don't want any kind of relationship with you, professional or personal.'

'And the child?'

'You will grant me sole custody.'

He nearly laughed. A choking bitter laugh that caught in his throat and burned. Because, no matter what she thought, in this moment he had no intention of letting either her or their child go. And if she thought he'd let his plans for Vladimir's company go, then she was sorely mistaken about the kind of man he was. Nothing would stop him from either goal, not her conditions, and certainly not her feeble attempt to coerce him into breaking the promise he'd made to his mother on her deathbed. The promise to dismantle every single piece of that damned company.

But Roman also knew that simply giving in to her demands would appear too easy—and although he had once thought his wife naïve and innocent, she was most definitely not stupid.

'If you have conditions, then so do I. If I travel for work, then I want you with me.'

'And if I travel for work? I have a fledging business that will require a lot of international travel.'

'What is this business?'

'Do you need to know?'

'In so much as you seem to need to know about most of my reasoning.'

'It's the one I told you about before,' she said, not having to explain what 'before' meant to either of them. Before they were married, before Ella had become pregnant. *Before* he had revealed his true self.

'You've done it?'

'Yes. Well…started to,' and Roman couldn't help but respond to the spark of pride and excitement in Ella's eyes. He recognised it, had seen it in his mother's eyes when she would sometimes dance for him, beneath the stars in the night sky. 'Célia is at the offices now—they're being set up as we speak,'

Ella pressed on, drawing him back from memories of the past. 'So I will need to be in Paris.'

'And I will need to be in Moscow,' he growled, chafing against the demand in her tone.

He watched as Ella valiantly struggled with her own anger. The flame of it lit her eyes and flushed her cheeks and for a moment he was back in that bed three months before and gripped by the arousal that had plagued him ever since, in spite of the shocking revelation that had seemed to change his life in an instant. In spite of the mental decree he had placed on himself never to touch Ella in such a way again. Possessiveness cut him to the quick. Her body, cradling the life they had created, was somehow even more appealing to him, and he felt every inch the beast he knew himself to be. He wanted her with a fierceness that stunned him. The need to taste her on his tongue, to feel her beneath his hands and body was now almost painful.

'If we can't figure even this out, then what kind of hope do we have?'

Her words drew him out of the sensual haze he found himself in and he forced his mind to broach the practicalities of the situation.

'Do you have any clients yet?'

'We're in the process of—'

'That's a no,' he concluded, perhaps more harshly than necessary. 'While I have not one, but two businesses based in Russia.'

'I appreciate that but, of the two of us, who will be least exhausted by travelling between the two places? I can barely even make it to the shops.'

'Should you even be working then?'

'Do not even suggest that this pregnancy would undermine—'

'Not what I meant, Ella,' he cut in before her ire could reach its full strength. 'Fine. I'll relocate to France, but we can't stay in your friend's apartment. I will need to return to Russia to wrap up a few things, but I'll be back with a list of properties we will visit.'

'I am perfectly happy to start looking myself.'

He ignored her as he pressed on to the one thought he simply couldn't rid himself of.

'And my one last condition is that you will share my bed.'

'Oh, please,' she scoffed, but the sound was only half able to disguise the true response he could see flaring in her eyes, in the way she hid from his gaze, in the way that her pulse kicked at the edges of her jawline.

'Ella, you demanded that I not lie to you. And yet you would try to lie to me in this?' he demanded. 'I would perhaps forgive you your inexperience that night, and the fact you have no comparison, so let me tell you. What we shared that night was unique.' Her gaze snapped up to his, as if she was shocked by his words. A shock that he felt every single time he thought of it, of being surrounded by her, of her body tightening around his, simply by their joining.

'And if you are demanding that you know me, if you want to see the truth of me, then you must have it all.'

At least, he promised himself, until the insane attraction that blazed through him the night they'd conceived their child was spent, was rid from his system. But until then he intended to indulge every possible moment he could have of it.

His words shocked Ella. The vague ideas she'd had of them sharing a living space but being able to retreat to their own privacy of an evening disappearing in the haze of smoke created by his demand. Because she had wondered whether that night had been... *normal*—it had been impossibly wondrous to her but perhaps it might have been almost habitual to him. But his words, the sincerity ringing in his eyes, the intensity as he somehow managed to bring forth her own intoxicating attraction and desire for him, they soothed as much as they aroused, linking them both on a level field of need and want. One that she'd craved and battled since leaving his bed.

'You agree?' he demanded from her silence.

She nodded, unable to speak past the sensual web he'd woven around her with a few simple words and a heated glance. But, despite the arrow of desire hitting a mark deep within her chest, she agreed because she desperately wanted to make this work. Their child was innocent and she wanted more for it than what they had had, more than the constant repetition of a cycle of vengeance that had brought them here.

She watched as he stood up from the sofa, his tall frame unfolding and stalking, with a lithe grace he must have inherited from his mother, towards the kitchenette. She frowned as he took the manila envelope in his hands and slid out the paperwork that contained only one signature.

Casting aside the envelope, he turned to Ella and slowly, and most definitely deliberately, tore the papers in two.

And all Ella could do was hope upon hope that he wouldn't do the same with her heart.

CHAPTER SEVEN

*'Cast your clothes into the fire, Red Riding Hood,
for there is no need for them any more, said the
wolf. Neither clothes nor lies will separate us. I
will be all that you could ever need.'*
        The Truth About Little Red Riding Hood
                                    —Roz Fayrer

AS ROMAN MANOEUVRED the sleek car that had been
waiting for him on the tarmac of the private airstrip
just outside of Toulouse around the small winding
roads that sadly did not take up enough of his concentration he wanted to curse. Ever since Ella had
demanded that he give up his plans to dismantle
Vladimir's business it had thrown everything into
disarray. For what felt like his entire life he'd had
but one goal. Even his grandfather's death hadn't
prevented him from wanting to ensure that the company that had meant more to Vladimir than his own
daughter was wiped from the face of the planet.

But now? He was going to be a father. A husband.
A *true* husband.

He'd meant what he'd said to Ella. He would do
anything to protect—to keep—his child. But a lifetime's pursuit of vengeance didn't stop on a dime.
Nor did a lifetime of being a lone wolf. Which was
why he was in the middle of this latest argument
with his wife.

'You just bought it?' she demanded from the pas-
senger seat beside him. 'Without giving me the opportunity of seeing it, of making my own decision?'

She was working herself into quite a state and he
couldn't really see what the problem was.

'What if *I'd* just gone out and bought a house?'

'Then we'd simply have two houses which we
could either keep or sell. And, either way, it's moot
because you didn't go out and buy a house.'

'No, *you* did. Without me knowing.'

'Ella, if you don't like it then we'll sell it. It's not
a big thing.'

'It's a house. Of course it's a big thing! It's completely wasteful.'

'You haven't even seen it yet.'

This was why he preferred being alone. There was
no one to question, to interrogate, second-guess or
disagree with his decisions. He simply did what he
wanted. It had been that way ever since he had escaped the clutches of his fourth foster home at the age
of sixteen. None of the foster parents had been able

to deal with a determinedly independent child who refused to listen to their rules. Even worse had been their attempts to break through the armour he had created around his heart. Nor had they been able to tackle a mind so quick and so intelligent they could barely keep up with his train of thought.

Looking back, he'd almost preferred the last couple, who had made their intentions clear. They didn't want to see or hear from him, only to accept the maintenance cheque they'd collected at the end of each month. It was certainly better than the first couple, who had *seemed* to want him and professed to take him into their hearts, but had persistently turned a blind eye to the fact their natural son had hated him with such a passion that Roman had been lucky to only suffer a bloody nose and black eye.

If it hadn't been for one of his teachers, sensing the fierce intelligence hidden behind a fair amount of bluster and anger—Roman ruefully admitted to himself—he might never have found his way into the invaluable scholarship programme that had led him to America. Ilyasov had been the first person, aside from his mother, who had seemed to genuinely want nothing from him. Because while his grandfather had *seemed* to want nothing from him, Roman knew that he had been the stick Vladimir had used to beat his daughter.

And the moment Roman had realised that he'd understood true power. True desire. To be able to identify or, better, *create* that which someone felt they wanted most in the world and to be the provider of that want…that was true control.

And while Roman hadn't been able or desirous of creating such a want in his wife, not yet at least, he knew from his time spent as her fiancé—the other *him*—what she wanted from a home. At the time he'd entertained it without really realising that it had struck a chord in him. It was as if she had focused her future as much on her imaginary house as he had on his path of vengeance. And as much as she might protest, he knew, with a certainty that had driven him to pay almost twice the asking price, that she would love the house he had found for her. For them. A them that would, in six months' time, include a small baby. A tiny, living, breathing part of him, of Ella, who would only have them to protect it, to put it first. A tiny baby whose equally tiny fist had already grasped his heart in its clutches.

Ella knew she was being unreasonable…to a point. She would love to have excused it as hormones from the pregnancy, but she knew she couldn't. Neither could she fault Roman's efficiency. Within three weeks he had apparently wrapped up enough of his business to take the time to find a property for them to share. And what had she done? Buried herself in her fledgling business. Choosing to ignore the way Roman and her future with him seemed to loom over her. Instead attempting to reach out to more international business contacts who might want to offset some of their income and guilt by aligning with the charities that Célia had already brought to the table.

It might have struck her as a little strange that Célia, who seemed to positively shrink at the prospect of interacting with billionaires and business-people, was happy to reveal her inner core of strength and persuasiveness with the other half of their intent. Célia seemed to know everything and anything about the international charities she drew to their company, and planned to entwine them with Ella's contacts, which was why the Venn diagram symbol on their business cards worked so well.

But in the short time since she'd last seen Roman, all Ella had been able to do was get Ivan Mozorov vaguely interested in a potential meeting. And she hated that her husband's apparent efficiency seemed to make her feel…inadequate. As if she was failing. Had already failed.

She'd gone to his club the night of the funeral to ensure her freedom and only succeeded in tying herself to Roman in the most fundamental of ways. And as much as she'd hoped for a different future for them both, the fact that she was being driven to see a house he had already bought, already planned for them to share, proved to her that once again Roman was doing things without her knowledge. That, no matter what he said, he hadn't changed at all. And

the fierce wave of uncertainty caused by that realisation made her feel awkward and a little panicky.
And guilty. Most awfully guilty, because she hated
herself for the fact that all she'd wanted was to be
free and now she felt trapped by him.

Roman guided the car down a dirt track in between sprawling, undulating fields. On one side an
industrious farmer was hard at work slicing down
the wheat, leaving tracks behind him that reminded
Ella oddly of Van Gogh's paintings. On the other
side dark green cloudlike trees gathered between
brief glimpses of a small terracotta-coloured town
in the distance sitting against the pale outline of the
looming Pyrenees.

It was the sight of the mountains slashed against
the horizon, as if painted in watercolours, that poked
and prodded at her memory. Of before. Before she'd
known the truth of him. And once again Ella felt the
loss of that man. Her fiancé. The one she had trusted
implicitly before he'd revealed himself to be false.
The one who had drawn from her unconscious the
very things that she had wanted most. A child, a husband, a family. She was then struck with the painful
irony that she now, in fact, had those things.

But she had not wanted them this way. Not with
this man and not under these circumstances.

Resentment roared within her, but was it really
her husband that was directed towards or her own
naivety? She honestly couldn't say any more.

Ella was about to launch into another verbal attack when they rounded an old stone wall and slowed before a set of wrought-iron gates. Even Dorcas poked her head up from the back seat, as if knowing that something of great interest lay beyond. The gates slowly inched open, as if purposely teasing the car's occupants before revealing the treasures that lay ahead.

The gravel driveway flicked up stones and crunched beneath the wheels of the car and she felt, with some not so small satisfaction, Roman flinch each time his precious paintwork came under attack. Then she caught sight of the sprawling converted farmhouse that sat at the top of the driveway.

And in the same way she had taken one look at the man to whom she was married and known that he would break her heart, she knew, *knew*, that this beautiful creamy-stoned estate was everything she'd ever wanted. Everything she'd once told Roman she wanted.

And for some inexplicable reason that made her want to cry.

Dorcas whined in the back seat of the car as if sensing the conclusion of their journey, scratching against the leather and causing Roman to wince again. *Good dog*, she mentally praised her as she blinked away the gathering tears pressing against her eyelids.

Ella looked up at the two-storey building stretching across and beyond the top of the driveway. Several outbuildings loomed in the distance, drawing her gaze beyond the estate, down a sloping bank of grass and across to the forest, where sunlight glinted against a copper dome she couldn't quite fathom.

'It is the gazebo down by the spring-fed lake that borders the property lines.'

The gentle tones of a French-accented female drew Ella's gaze back to the property with a snap. Expecting to meet the stranger's eyes, Ella frowned as she took in the immaculately dressed woman who apparently had directed her statement to the man who would naturally have known what his money had bought.

'Dominique Delvaux,' she said with a feline smile, directed at her husband. 'I am the estate's *guardienne*.'

Ella just about managed to restrain the growl she felt vibrating within her throat. Dorcas, apparently, had no such self-control as a low warning rumbled from the beast in spite of the look of disdain the beautiful Frenchwoman cast in the dog's direction.

Ella looked down at her clothes, creased and crumpled and slightly damp from the journey, despite the powerful air-conditioning that had at first sent shivers across her skin. At the time, Ella had allowed herself that small lie, pretending her body's reaction had nothing to do with the impossibly handsome man beside her.

A handsome man whose charms were apparently not wasted on the *guardienne*. Ella had dressed for comfort, where Ms Delvaux seemed to have dressed for a fashion show. And now, as she looked at the other woman, she felt the slightly tight press of the waistband of her linen trousers and wished that she had listened to Célia's suggestion that she think about purchasing a new wardrobe for her slowly developing bump.

She followed her husband as the *guardienne* beckoned them into the building and the enticing cool interior of the hallway. A small table by the entrance held a jug of water with cucumber, mint and ice, the white linen tablecloth beneath soaking up the condensation forming on the glass. Ms Delvaux filled two glasses and Ella nearly smiled as decorum finally won out over desire and the other woman offered her a glass before her husband.

'Merci,' Ella said overly graciously, while taking the glass with one hand and gently pressing her other to her abdomen, unnecessarily soothing the almost indistinguishable shape beginning to form there. The *guardienne*'s eyes snapped back and forth between Ella's hand and face and Ella practically preened under the dawning realisation she could read in the other woman's face.

Message received and understood, Ms Delvaux retreated into professionalism and began to outline the impressive attributes of the house.

'The main building dates from the seventeenth century, when it was the heart of a growing estate. The charmingly renovated façade reveals large and light interiors. As you can see, the dramatic ninety square metre reception hall has a grand fireplace—

as does the master suite on the floor above at the other end of the house. It is one of seven bedrooms and the restoration brought about an additional two bathrooms, bringing the number to five. Below you'll find a garage and a generous wine cellar...'

Ella let the woman's voice recede into the background as she drifted off into the large living area she could see on the left, Dorcas nuzzling her hand and keeping her company while her husband and the *guardienne* remained behind in the *'dramatic ninety square metre reception hall'*. It *was* impressive, but it made her only think of Vladimir's hall, the one she had spun in the night that Roman had revealed his deceit.

But all thoughts of that night fled under the beautiful streams of light filtering in from the windows as she took in the soothing cream tones of the living area, centred around an incredible fireplace that she thought she might actually be able to stand within. Two sprawling sofas stood sentinel either side of it and the terracotta stone flooring beckoned her further into the large room. Rounding a corner, she came to a stunning open-plan kitchen, connected by beautiful aged oak beams running across the ceiling, giving the space a warmth and cosiness despite its size. Utility rooms sprang off to the side, her eyes eating up every inch of the incredible space.

She looked to Roman, sensing the heat of his gaze. The smug look of satisfaction across his features at having recognised that she'd fallen in love with the house took the wind out of her sails somewhat.

Ella approached the staircase and moved through the rooms slowly, as if scared that she'd miss something or move too quickly, in case it would all disappear. It was everything she'd ever wanted. There was enough to remind her of her grandmother's cottage, a homeliness and simplicity that could only be afforded by extreme wealth. A wealth that her husband had brought to bear against her. Or for her? She simply couldn't tell any more.

She felt overwhelmed, confused and strangely hurt by the fact that he'd found a home that was almost straight out of the fantasies she'd discussed during their engagement. Because she was desperately trying to see Roman as two different men—the fantasy she had fallen for and the man who had destroyed all that she had known. But this blurred the lines—this confused her because it meant that she could not keep them separate. She loved the house immediately and her heart ached. Because it meant that she would have to admit that he knew her. He knew her well enough to give her this house—her dream house. But, more importantly, *she* didn't know *him* at all.

Roman dismissed the overly attentive *guardienne* and, as he waited for Ella to return from inspecting the rooms upstairs, he stood in the living room, trying to imagine what his life would look like in a

month's time, a year's time, five years' time even.
Would there be a child's toys scattered about this
room? Would there be the subtle touches of Ella on
the walls and in the rooms as she placed her own
mark upon the house? And what traces would there
be of him? Would there, his inner voice questioned,
be *any* trace of him?

His thoughts were cut off as he heard the click
of Ella's heels coming down the staircase. And suddenly he didn't want to look, didn't want to know
what she thought of the house he had conjured from
the descriptions she had given him during their engagement. Because if he had got it wrong…

But when he turned he saw neither love nor disappointment. No. His wife surprised him yet again
with her anger.

'What is wrong?' he demanded, his voice rough
and guttural, resisting the urge to run his hands
through his hair in frustration. He had been so sure
of it. So sure of her.

'Nothing,' she said bitterly, causing him to frown.
'Absolutely nothing is wrong with it. You've apparently thought of everything.'

'And that is a bad thing?'

She glared at him mulishly. And suddenly he
wanted nothing more than to kiss away that anger, to
use it, to bend it to his will. But he couldn't. Because
she was his wife and she deserved more than that.
Even if she was glaring at him with a strange com-

bination of anger, resentment and hurt. The former he could handle, the latter not so much. Because he was beginning to think that even a lifetime's worth of compensation wouldn't atone for his sins. Sins he was apparently still committing, though he couldn't quite fathom what this one could have been.

'Words,' he bit out.

'What?'

'You're going to have to use them to tell me what I've done wrong this time.'

She scowled again and Dorcas chose wisely to vacate the room. For there was a storm brewing, one of quite spectacular proportions if he wasn't mistaken. One he felt echoing in his own chest for release.

'I...' she said as she paced the length of the room and then turned on her heel. 'You...' she said, trying again, as if she were afraid of what would be released if she lifted the lid on the ferocity of what she was clearly struggling with.

'Ella,' he warned. 'If you try to keep all that in—'

'I don't think you want to know. Truly,' she ground out.

'I know how damaging anger can be. How it can scorch you from the inside out and twist every last good thing in you and make you dark, make you... vengeful.' And suddenly it was the most important thing to him. He wanted, *needed*, to hear whatever it was she had to say, because it was killing him to see the beautiful, innocent, joyful young woman so tormented.

'It's perfect. It's absolutely everything I ever wanted. Everything that I never knew I wanted until I met a man in the woods and he offered me a future I had yet to realise I desperately sought.'

She turned away from him, trying to hide the overwhelming ache that beat in her chest. An ache borne from the past, into the present and a future she now feared she'd never have. But Roman was right, she did need to find the words to explain...to release this overwhelming *hurt*.

'I was young when I lost my parents. Five. Too young to articulate what I was feeling, too young to understand Vladimir when he tried to explain that my parents were never coming back. That I'd be living with him now. Too young to understand why everything hurt and why I could not stop playing with the doll's house and the small wooden figures of two parents and a child. Why in my mind I had them eat dinner together every day. Why the mother and father used to tuck their child into bed each night and read her stories.

'As much as you might hate to hear it, Vladimir *did* look after me, but mostly he was focused on material needs. And then with my grandmother... Summers with her were magical. Truly. But she was an older woman—she had raised her child and had buried her. She loved me completely, but she wasn't exactly a suitable companion for a child. I spent more time in the woods alone, looking for fairies, hiding in the bushes, running after birds and the rabbits. I was…' Ella twisted her hands before her, unaccountably ashamed of admitting her loneliness as if it were a mark against her perfect grandmother. 'I was isolated. There were no children to play with, all of them already with school friends or away for their own summer holidays.'

And somewhere in those months, those long stretching summer days, she had formed an idea of her future. One that she now both had and didn't have. She turned back to Roman, who was watching her, his usually bright eyes a deeper stormy blue.

'When I met my fiancé in the woods he offered me everything I had always wanted. Companionship, someone to confide in, someone with whom I could have the very thing I'd always wanted, ever since it had been ripped away from me at the age of five. A home, a family.

'You, Roman. You offered me my fantasy and this? This is too close and yet so far from what I wanted.'

'Fantasies aren't real.'

'Like your fantasy of revenge?' she couldn't help but taunt. 'It's not the house, Roman. It's the fact that after all these years, all the things I wanted…it's so nearly there, but I can't help but feel that I'm going to be just as lonely as I once was in the woods. Just as lonely in this perfect house.'

She dared to cast a look at him then, hoping beyond hope that he'd reassure her, that he'd have words and compassion to make all her fears disappear. His whole body stilled—as if he were made of marble, as if he too realised how important his answer would be, what she was really asking him, the truth behind her words, the question.

'Ella,' he said, shaking his head, 'I don't want to make promises I cannot keep.' She huffed out a cynical breath, and he pushed on. 'There have clearly been enough of those between us. But you are pregnant with my child. You are my wife. You are not in this alone, not if you don't choose to be. When I am not in this house I will be at the other end of the phone any time, *any time* you need me. I'll fly back in a heartbeat if you desire it. And if you feel that my business in Russia takes me too much away from you then we will visit that if and when you choose. But Ella, that is not what is really upsetting you,' he stated with determined simplicity, the glints of gold in his eyes firing against the blue. As if he were made of the stuff. As if he had steeled himself for an answer he already knew.

She cursed and stalked from the room, paying no heed to the lithe graceful strides that caught up to her in a heartbeat, her exit halted by the hand at her wrist, spinning her back round to almost crash against the hard chest looming over her.

'No. It's not,' she said, finally owning up to the truth of what she really feared in that moment. 'It's you,' she said, punctuating the statement with a strike against his powerful chest. 'I don't trust you. You took away the only solid, stable things I had in my life. You took away a loving guardian and replaced him with a Machiavellian monster, uncaring, unfeeling and manipulative. You took away the man I wanted to spend the rest of my life with, a man I had fallen in love with, a man I shared my hopes and dreams for a future with. How on earth am I supposed to believe that you won't take this away from me now? How am I supposed to trust you?'

Roman wanted to argue with his wife's words, deny them as lies, but couldn't. She had been badly used by both Vladimir and himself. And while he'd tried to explain it to himself as just, as necessary for his pursuit of revenge, with the damage from his actions clear to see before him, he could no longer fight the awful truth of what he had done. That all the power and incredible self-possession he had seen the night they had conceived their child had been a thin layer of newly formed defence against the deeper devastation he had wrought on this extraordinary woman. He cursed himself to hell and back, lashing himself mentally with a thousand different painful thoughts. But this wasn't about him, not here and now. It was about Ella. And what she needed.

'I wanted to show you, with this house, that you can have whatever you want most in the world.'

'But that is the problem. You know what it is that

I want because you got the truth out of me when we were engaged…and I did not do the same. You know me, but I don't know you. All I know is that you have taken decisions that I would want to have made myself away from me. You have…'

'Taken away your freedom.'

She nodded sadly as she bit into the lower lip he wanted for himself and then castigated himself once again for his inappropriate wayward thoughts.

'I am not used to having others to think of,' he admitted roughly. 'So much of my life has been lived under my own direction, my own decisions. But that will change. I do understand why you feel this way. And I know that I am the cause of it. But, if you let me, I will prove that you can trust me. I will not take those decisions away from you again. I promise you that.' He held her gaze with his, determined to allow her to see the truth, the honesty of his words, hoping beyond all hope that he could honour that promise.

'And you are right. I did see the truth of you before. Not just the innocence and naivety I once taunted you with, but the strength of a woman who cared deeply about her grandmother. So much so that she would put her own dreams on hold. A woman determined not to rely on the money provided by her guardian and father, who would not fritter it away on silly ephemeral comforts but create a business that would provide much needed support for charities throughout the globe. And even after events that would have cowed a great many other people, a woman who found her own strength and determination to ask for what she wanted, to demand what she was due. And that woman was incredible to me. Empowered and enthralling enough to make me beg her to take what she wanted from me and leave me wanting more. A woman who will make the most wonderful mother, caring, honest and with an integrity that leaves me ashamed,' he admitted.

'But you have to decide whether you can trust me. Because, if you don't, then you will never stop second-guessing me and it will drive you mad,' he concluded. Just like it had driven Roman almost mad in those first few months after his mother's death—wondering, questioning whether he could have done something— anything more to save her. He could not, and would not, allow Ella to live under such a damaging weight.

He produced the keys to the house from his pocket. 'This is the only set of keys to this house. The deeds are in your name and no one else's. It is yours. Completely. You can do with it what you will. Sell it, rent it, keep it.' He pressed the keys into her hands. 'I'll wait outside until you're ready to leave.'

Ella felt the loss of him from the house as something physical. The hurt, angry part of her cried that she would never be able to trust him. But the softer yearning part of her looked about a house almost made from her dreams and hoped. Roman was right.

She had to stop. She had to draw a line under the past if they had any hope of the future.

As Roman had painted the picture of her as he had seen her, Ella had wavered, wanting to be all that he described. Hoping that he was speaking the truth and feeling something unfurl within her, reaching to be that person. Instead of using her fears against her, he had listened to them, comforted them and her. She looked around the room, seeing with hope what her future could be. And for the first time in a long time she felt strong enough to reach for it.

But within that strength was a deep knowledge, a belief. She might be able to trust her husband with this, but she would never trust him with her heart. Could never. Because that hurt would be too much to bear.

As she left the house she saw Roman sitting on the steps leading down to the driveway, Dorcas lifting her head from her master's touch in happy expectation. The tableau was oddly moving. Her dog, her husband, her home.

'So what else does our lovely new estate have to offer?' she asked him, the ache in her chest easing just a little as she saw the answering smile in his gaze.

CHAPTER EIGHT

And now every bite, every snarl, every gnashing of his teeth was about to be heaped on the wolf tenfold. For the one thing he had not learned yet was that you can never escape the actions of the past.

The Truth About Little Red Riding Hood
—Roz Fayrer

ELLA FINISHED THE phone call to Célia with a smile on her face, having gone over the details ahead of the meeting with Ivan Mozorov. In the last few weeks they'd found more interested parties and Ella could now sense the way their business would begin to take off. Célia had sent photos of the office in Paris that was a few days away from being not only fully functioning but very beautiful.

She and Roman had settled into a routine of sorts. Roman would spend the middle three days of the week in Russia, Monday and Friday commuting, and would stay in France with her at the weekend.

And, despite what he'd said about sharing his bed, he hadn't enforced the decree, which had—at first—made Ella feel a sense of relief. But as the days wore on…she became dissatisfied. She rolled her shoulders at the thought of it, as if shaking off some inner sense of frustration. She couldn't help the feeling that she was waiting for the other shoe to drop, only it felt less like a shoe and more like the sword of Damocles.

Her body, thankfully having moved past the morning sickness stage, had begun to blossom. She'd never thought she'd enjoy pregnancy but at the moment she was relishing the new freedom in her body. Their child was now about the size of a pea pod, the doctor had explained, which had caused her to refer to her baby as Sweetpea. And each day she marvelled at the subtle changes happening, the new gentle curves of her body. A body that Roman seemed intent on ignoring for the most part.

It was as if now that Roman had given her the space to relax, to ease into the situation and the house, she couldn't escape him, her thoughts of him and the ecstasy of what they had shared that night. It made her feel…wanton, and slightly obsessed. She had begun to dress each day with Roman in mind, trying to tempt him into something he suddenly seemed to think was inappropriate.

When she wasn't lusting after her husband she was delighting in the house he had found for them. It was close enough to visit her grandmother and a short flight to Paris for when the offices were up and running. And although she had visited her grandmother several times, Ella found herself not quite wanting to leave the beautiful home.

There was simply too much to see and discover about this place. After breakfast in the morning she and Dorcas would roam the sprawling acreage down to the freshwater spring that wound across the border of their lands and she couldn't have stopped Dorcas diving into it for a moment because the pure joy in the dog's eyes made her laugh, and soothed some of the past hurts.

But her favourite part of the estate was the stone gazebo with the copper domed roof. Every day she reached for the almost grey pillars, placing her hands against the cool stone, wondering who might have done so in the years before. She enjoyed imagining the different women who might have stood there looking out over the same view, generation after generation, feeling a strange kinship with them.

She wondered what they might think of her choices in the house, the few small personal touches she had brought to the already incredible spaces. She had claimed an office from one of the bedrooms, which Roman had insisted on filling with state-of-the-art technology, eager to provide whatever material need she could think of. But it had left the stark difference between the material and the emotional even clearer to Ella. For while on paper everything

Roman did was perfect, was the epitome of the doting husband, it didn't quite feel like *him*.

Ella left her office and made her way to the bedroom she had been using. Because that was how she found herself thinking of it. A room that she was using until she finally took up residence with her husband in *his* room. She opened the wardrobe, scanning her eyes over the new dresses she had bought, picking out the one that she had chosen for tonight's meeting with Ivan Mozorov in Paris. And her eye caught on the red cloak her fiancé had bought just over a year ago.

And while Ella had been too fearful of shaking the still fragile foundations of what they were building together, could not quite bring herself to question it, to question him, she couldn't help but wonder whether this might be the jolt they needed. The memory, reminder of what they had been, and hope for what they could be.

As the small private jet banked to the left to come in to land at the small private airfield just outside of Toulouse, Roman rubbed a hand over his face, trying to erase the exhaustion he was sure was now visible. It had to be, because he felt it in every single inch of his body.

Maintaining two fully functioning businesses was surprisingly difficult as, despite the efficient team he had brought into Kolikov Holdings to do a full audit, his grandfather's business had accrued a little more than its sterling reputation over the years. It had accrued debts. And the steel fortress around his heart tightened at the thought that the old bastard really had had the last laugh.

Roman wanted nothing more than to tear it to shreds, but the promise he'd made to Ella... It had him warring with an instinct that had been honed over nearly eighteen years, and a desire to be better, to do better, to give her what it was she wanted. And if that came at the cost of what *he* wanted? That was why he'd had two proposals drawn up by his team. One for liquidation and one for a complete overhaul.

But, he ruefully admitted to himself, it wasn't just that. His exhaustion stemmed mostly from the fact that he hadn't had a decent night's sleep for even one night in the estate he shared with Ella. Knowing that she was along the hall, knowing that he hadn't enforced the sleeping arrangements he'd crassly thrown at her in a fit of pique, was undoing him.

And when he wasn't thinking about the ecstasy that only his wife had brought him he was wondering what kind of father he would be. His own father had abandoned him, Vladimir had been a cruel, manipulative piece of work and the foster homes afterwards not much better. Until now, he'd embraced a solitary path, a ruthless pursuit of single-minded vengeance. What if he betrayed his child? What if he betrayed Ella? All these thoughts were sneaking in under the

defences of a certainty that usually protected his conscience. The certainty that he was doing the right
thing. Though he knew that generating two plans for
two different futures was not *'doing the right thing'*.
Not for Ella, anyway.

Slamming the door on the car that had brought
him home, he closed the door on the fears he refused
to expose to his wife. Dorcas was standing guard
at the door, wagging her tail furiously but clearly
knowing better than to pounce on him. Unaccountably, something in his chest eased to see the animal
so happy at his arrival.

As he entered the hallway he ground to a halt at
the sight of his wife, at the large mirror by the side
table, putting in her earrings. It was such a simple
gesture, so simply domestic, that it took him a moment to realise that she was dressed in a stunning
creation that shone beneath the lights in the hall.

The bodice that encased her chest was made up of
thousands of folds of pale pink chiffon, all meeting
to twist in the centre of her breasts, drawing his hungry gaze to the perfection they hid. The cap sleeves,
dotted with crystals, perched on her shoulders as if
almost about to fall, illuminating the length of her
collarbone and the beautiful curve of her neck. The
material gathered beneath a band at her waist, and
plunged to the floor in swathes of silk.

The beauty of his wife undid him completely, rob-

bing him of speech or thought—at least any thought
other than *mine*.

She turned to him then, head still bent, fiddling
with an earring, and frowned. A look of hurt passed
across her features, which she vainly tried to hide.
Turning back to the mirror, she said, 'You have forgotten.'

Honestly, Roman would have replied that he'd forgotten his own name until he caught sight of the invitation on the table and something cold and hard
gripped his gut.

'The ballet,' he said, his tone completely devoid
of emotion.

'The meeting with Ivan Mozorov,' she clarified.
'Apparently he enjoys mixing pleasure with business,
and has generously graced me with the period of the
interval to make my pitch.' She turned back to him,
having won the battle over her earring. 'It's okay,'
she said, shaking her head in a way that clearly indicated it was anything but, 'you can stay—'

'I just need ten minutes,' Roman said, stalking
past his wife and towards his room and the shower,
desperate to wash off the cold sweat that had gathered at the nape of his neck.

Not for a minute did he think Ella had realised
what she had done, what that would do to him. And,
for the first time he could remember, that hurt.

His muscles ached as he climbed the staircase
towards the bedroom. He pulled off his jacket and

threw it on the bed, he struggled with the cufflinks at his wrists and toed off his shoes. All these things were done automatically and blindly. Because, in his mind's eye, he saw his mother staring at the small black and white television set in the small room they shared as she watched her old ballet company perform for the Russian president. He saw her round, wide unblinking eyes fill with a sheen of tears still yet to be shed. Even as a child, he'd heard her unspoken thoughts.

That could have been me. That should *have been me.*

His touch, his attempted hug, his words of love hadn't been enough to pull her from the trance-like way she had watched every second of the performance.

And that had been the one and only time he'd ever seen the ballet. Before tonight.

The Palais Garnier in Paris was breathtaking. The nineteenth-century opera house was a glory of pillars and arches, flanked by two magnificent golden statues proclaiming the beauty of the building. If Ella had been awed by the exterior of the building, the interior was almost too much. Stunning marble flooring reached to the dual arched staircases, at the bottom of which two female allegories held torches as if to guide the visitor onwards and upwards.

As they took their seats in the box that Célia had somehow arranged for her and her husband, Ella scanned the auditorium in the vain hope that she might be able to catch sight of Ivan before the interval. The hushed whispers of the audience rose up from below, inciting a low thrum of excitement within her—not just for the business meeting but because she had not been to the ballet for years.

How much had changed since she'd last seen a performance. Vladimir now gone from her life, she now married and about to be a mother herself. But Ella forced her mind back to the task at hand. She wasn't here for this performance, but one of her own. To secure their first client. It had meant so much to her that Roman hadn't cried off and had come with her. Although, casting a glance to where her husband sat, grim-faced and clench-jawed, she wondered if perhaps it would have been better if he had stayed behind.

Just as she worked up the courage to ask him if he was okay, the orchestra began their warm up and an expectant hush descended. The lights in the auditorium dimmed and soon Ella was lulled into the beautiful and heartbreaking story of *Giselle*.

By the time that the curtain came up for the interval Ella's heart ached and the tissue clutched in her hand was damp from the tears that she had swept away from sight. But she thrust all thoughts aside as she now had to focus on Ivan and her business.

Roman shook his head when she asked if he wanted to accompany her, his focus zeroed in on the empty stage. If she'd had more presence of mind, if she hadn't been so distracted by her own focus, she might have entreated him to explain, might have wondered what had happened to cast her husband in such a dark aura. But she hadn't and as she went in search of Ivan she instead only felt the thrill of the chase, the hope and expectation that she would secure her and Célia's first client.

'Come on, darling.'

It was his mother's voice, not Ella's, that Roman heard when she returned to him.

'Let's go.' Ella's clipped words cut through the memories that had shrouded him the moment he'd remembered where she'd wanted to go that evening. As if his mind had worked against him, had purposely chosen to forget that they were to attend the ballet.

He frowned, his mind taking a moment to catch up with what Ella had just stated.

'Go?'

'Yes. I… I want to go.'

'What happened with Ivan?' he asked as he stood up and was practically hauled from the box, out into the hallway mid-performance and out to the waiting car that would take them to the helicopter he'd arranged to fly them back home.

'Nothing.'

'Nothing?'

'Are you going to repeat everything I say?' she asked, the bitterness on her tongue nothing compared to the glittering tears he could see gathering in the corners of her eyes.

'But I've heard your pitch, it was faultless. He would have been mad to turn it down.'

'It wasn't a problem with the business plan,' she said, her head turned away from him as they slipped into the limousine.

'Then—'

'You.'

'What?' he asked, outraged.

'Ivan was deeply apologetic, but he simply wouldn't do business with the wife of the Great Wolf,' she concluded scathingly.

An almost savage fury roared within him—that he had been the cause of Ella's upset—and then he truly appreciated the irony within that thought. His mind quickly veered away from that to action, to purpose. Roman was more than willing and capable of tangling with anyone who would want to mess with him, but his wife? Oh, no. That would not stand.

'He will regret it,' Roman forced darkly through his teeth.

'Really? And what damage would that do to my business? You can't bully and cajole clients into working with me.'

'I will find someone for you,' he declared.

'No.'

'But—'

'I said no. I think you've done enough, don't you?'

Every single other question, suggestion or attempt to broach the shield around his wife was met with a withdrawn silence that cut him as deeply as the thought that he had been responsible for her failure.

By the time they had returned to the estate and he had watched Ella, all poise and elegance, retreat to her room, Roman felt as if he were fit to burst. Sleep would be impossible as fury had lined his veins like detonating cord and he needed to move, to walk off this energy that was almost sparking from his fingers.

Restlessness like he'd never known before spurred him out onto the sloping garden that led towards the stream and the forest. The darkness of the night shrouded him in a heady combination of past memories and present concerns. That he'd been the cause of Ella's failed business meeting ate at him, that the reputation he'd garnered in order to achieve his own ends with Vladimir had somehow directed Ella's future had caught him by the throat and the ache that formed there lodged into a solid, painful thing.

Ella hadn't been able to sleep. She'd tried, forcing herself to let go of the anger and frustration that had clouded her since being dismissed by Ivan. That it was not the business or the plan that he had objected to but the person she had married had infuriated her. Not for one moment had she placed the blame at Roman's door—but as she lay in bed she realised that was quite possibly what he thought.

No, she was furious that, once again, she had not been seen or valued in her own right, but as an attachment to someone else. A way to lash back at Roman for some prior reckoning that he had nothing to do with.

Only now, as flashes of the night before burst through her mind, did Ella realise that something had been wrong with Roman long before her business meeting with Ivan. Something she had failed to see at the time. Because the dark aura that had surrounded him belonged to neither her fiancé nor the man she seemed to have married. It was something strange and new and something she now desperately wanted to confront.

But his bed was empty, his room, the entire house, save for Dorcas, curled up on her bed in the corner of the landing. She had raised her head briefly as Ella had moved about the empty rooms and, apparently deciding that this was the business of humans, had promptly gone back to sleep.

Returning to the landing, Ella took in the view of the sloping garden, the forests, the copper domed gazebo glinting in the moonlight and the silver thread of the freshwater lake winding across the bottom of the garden like a slash upon the horizon. Although Ella hadn't seen a glimpse of him, she instinctively knew that he was out there. She ran back to her room and grabbed the first thing that came to hand—the red cloak—swept it around her shoulders and, with bare feet, slipped from the house and into the forest.

She found him sitting on the cold stone steps of

the gazebo, staring out into the distance, where a strange fog had begun to roll in off the Pyrenees, creating an odd sense of foreboding. For a moment she held her breath, taking in the sight of him— shirtsleeves rolled back, tie loose and hanging down either side of his collar, as motionless as the stone he sat upon.

The fall of his slightly long hair had been swept back from his forehead, his nose proud and jawline determined, clenched, as if warding back some great bank of emotions. It had been the same way he'd looked as she had snuck glances at him through the ballet that evening.

She heard him sigh, an exhalation of something more than just oxygen, an acknowledgement of her presence. Without a word, she stepped forward from the soft springy grass that had been merely damp with dew onto the solid frigid stone, sending shivers through her feet and legs all the way up her spine. Ignoring it, she took a seat beside him, leaving the smallest space between their bodies.

For a moment they stayed like that, the silence vibrating with unspoken words, a conversation of bodies, adjusting to the presence of another.

'So, do you come here often?' she ventured, regretting the crass joke almost the moment the words had come out of her mouth.

'Yes,' he replied after a breath, surprising her with his honesty.

'Really?'

'Yes,' he said, smiling gently into the night.

'I didn't know.'

'I… I've always found it slightly difficult to sleep, but…'

'It's been worse here?'

He nodded. Ella opened her mouth to ask why, but Roman pressed on.

'When I was younger—before my mother…' He stopped, seeming to begin again in a different time and place. 'After Vladimir cut off my mother, and she could no longer dance because she was pregnant with me, she was hired as a cleaner by a rich family in Voskresensk. They were a decent enough family, from what I could tell. But they had this garden that bordered the river there. And sometimes—more often after she became ill—she would wake me in the middle of the night, and bring me out under the stars to dance.'

As if he had conjured her from his memories, Roman could have sworn that he saw her that night. Dressed in a white cotton shift, moving beneath the stars, twirling pirouettes, the gentle sweep of her arms as they reached, yearning, probing the night air, dancing to music that only she could hear, the gentle footfalls and sweeps creating their own rhythm. He had sat there for hours, over hundreds of nights, and it was not enough, would never be enough. He would swap his soul to be sitting there, shivering in the cold and not minding it one bit, because it was the only time he'd ever seen his mother truly happy. Truly free.

'She was an incredible dancer. She had been the principal at the Utonchennyy Ballet Company. And the last performance she had with them before Vladimir cut her from his life was *Giselle*.'

From the corner of his eye he saw Ella raise her hand to her mouth as if to stifle some expression he wasn't sure either one of them wanted to acknowledge.

'What was she like?' Ella ventured after a while using hushed tones as if not wanting to break the gossamer-thin web around them.

'Sad,' Roman admitted. 'She was sad a lot of the time. It was hard for her, the life of a cleaner so different from the luxury that she had grown up in. I could see, even as a child, the wrench that she felt at not being able to give me more. The struggles she had, working and raising a child on her own. But the nights when she would bring me out were…they were enough for me.'

'I'm sorry. So sorry. If I'd known, I would never have asked you to come with me.'

Roman didn't do her the injustice of dismissing her apology. 'I know.'

'I wish I could have seen her dance.'

He smiled. Somehow, no matter how their wedding had come about, he knew that his mother would have liked Ella. The kindness in her, the goodness. All the things that he was not. That he had forced out of his breast the moment he had laid his mother to rest. And, for the first time ever, he feared that while his mother might have liked Ella, she might not have liked what her son had become.

'She would have been proud of what you have achieved,' Ella said as if she had somehow sensed his inner thoughts.

'But would she have been proud of me?' he said, finally giving voice to his fear.

For a moment he thought she might not answer, might not be able to find any redeeming quality within her husband.

Then he felt her small hand slip beneath his arm, winding him towards her, and her head lay on his shoulder as she leaned into him.

'She would have been proud of the man determined to raise his child with its mother. Proud of the man determined to give his wife the home she'd always wanted. She would have been proud of the man who comforted his wife when she felt lost.'

'Even if that man was the cause of his wife's insecurity?'

Ella nestled her head deeper into his shoulder. 'And proud of the man who would change his ways to try to be better for his wife and child. Because that's all we can do. Try.' She paused, as if working up towards something Roman feared might hurt.

Might cause an even greater ache in his chest. 'Earlier I said I was sorry for asking you to come to the ballet tonight. But I'm not,' she said, pulling back so that she could look at him, so that he could see the sincerity in her eyes. 'I'm not, because it brought us here. Because I now see a little of your mother.'

'I haven't thought about her dancing in years,' Roman admitted roughly.

'That is a shame. Because I want you to have those memories. I want you to talk about her, so that our child can know their grandmother. I don't have any real memories of my parents, only what Vladimir told me, and my grandmother told me. And I want you to be able to talk about Tatiana—share stories, anecdotes, memories that made you laugh and love, because that's what I want our child to be surrounded by.'

He looked at his wife for the first time, seeing her properly as she sat beside him, her cornflower-blue eyes large and round and her lips so red against the pale creamy skin lit by the stars, and he wanted to lose himself in her. Wanted to take what she was consciously or unconsciously offering. But he didn't feel as if he had that right. Didn't know if his touch, his kiss would be welcome after all the damage he had wrought. Not just the loss of a business deal, but long before then.

And as if she could sense his hesitation, sense the current of his thoughts, the need coursing through

him like wildfire, as if all this time, all these weeks
and months of frustration and want and desire, came
crashing about them in this one moment, she pulled
him to her and pressed her mouth against his in comfort, in her own need.

The passion she offered him, matched only by his
own, set light to his thoughts, to the hold of the past
and the uncertainty of the future. The moment her
lips opened to him, her tongue drawing his deeper
into their kiss, he was lost.

He spread the red cloak across the marble floor
of the stone gazebo, the crimson pooling about her
as he laid her back.

'This was what I saw when I bought this cloak,' he
admitted, desire painting his voice dark. 'Removing
it from you, revealing the beauty within.'

The thin cotton nightdress glowing in the star-
light made her angelic and him unworthy. 'I should
take you back to the house, to soft cotton sheets and
soft deep mattresses. You deserve more than this.'

More than he could offer.

She looked at him then, large crystal-blue eyes
wide and crimson mouth part opened on a breath.
'There is nowhere I'd rather be than here beneath
the stars with you.'

In a second Roman had claimed her lips with his,
and Ella felt an almost primal cry rise within her. A
cry of loss, of longing, of comfort, of desperation.

The sword that had hung above them for so long had dropped and severed the final barriers holding them both back as hands swept across bodies, tongues swept across teeth, lips across skin. She felt him draw up the cotton nightdress at her thighs, bunching it in his hands, both trapping her by the taut material and protecting her from him.

The peaks of her nipples pressing against the thin fabric refused to disguise her want and she no longer wanted to hide it. No longer wanted the power of her need to come from anger or resentment, or a yearning for the unknown. This time, she strove for something more. Because she knew that this night had cost them both and only their touch could offer comfort the way that words, yet, could not.

Her hands ran over his shirt, desperate to feel skin, wanting, needing more. As he pressed open-mouthed kisses against her neck, across her collarbone and further to between the V of her neck, she vainly struggled with the buttons on his shirt—the passion he wrought in her making her fingers clumsy and awkward.

His hands released her for the moment it took to haul the shirt over his head and discard it, as if equally impatient as she to be skin to skin, but instead of returning to the kiss he held himself back, hovering over her, as if consuming her with his gaze. There was something in it, something deep and dark, and she went to raise a hand of comfort to his hardened jaw. But he shook his head to warn her off.

'I... I don't even know if I can hope to be the man you should have by your side. You're making me want to, but...'

'You once asked me to trust you. And now I'm asking that of you. Trust me, because I know you can be. You *are*,' Ella said, feeling the truth of her words settling in her chest—a chest that ached for her husband, for the pain he had experienced, all that she could see he had sacrificed. A boy trying to avenge the death of his mother, a man trying to be better, do better. A man scared of opening himself up to what it was they were weaving between them.

He returned to their kiss as if he too understood the need to feel the purity of the connection they seemed only to share here, now.

Roman pushed up under her nightdress, his hands sliding over her thighs, the heat from his palms both soothing and torturous at the same time as each sweep moved closer and closer to where she wanted to feel him. She felt his fingers pull at the edges of her underwear, drawing them almost leisurely down her thighs and from her ankles.

Her fingers once again struggled with the belt on his trousers, only to find them thrust aside by Roman's efficient swift movements as he freed himself.

'Tell me you want this.' His words were more of

a plea than a demand. 'Tell me you're as lost to this as I am. Tell me—'

'I do, I am, and right now I'd tell you anything you want to hear if you would—'

All words, all coherent thought was lost as he thrust into her, the delicious smooth glide of him within her taking her by surprise and propelling her towards an edge that she felt far too close to. Her hands flew to his hips as he entered her again and again, wringing pleasure from her that she feared would never be satisfied, would never be appeased. But she had been wrong. Because almost against her will the world came crashing down about her as everything within her rose to reach out to it. Her body, heart and soul pushed and pulled in a million different directions, yet all coming back to one place, one thing... Roman.

CHAPTER NINE

*And for a brief moment Red Riding Hood was
happy. She was proud of the relationship she'd
forged with the wolf, proud of what she'd ac-
complished. But, as we all know, pride comes
before a fall, and Red Riding Hood couldn't see
the chasm before her. Only him. Only the wolf.*
        The Truth About Little Red Riding Hood
                                    —Roz Fayrer

ELLA HAD NEVER gone back to her room in the house.
Since the night of the ballet she had shared his bed,
waiting for him while he was away in Russia and
delighting in him as he returned to her in France.

And each time he did, he marvelled that what
had once been a small, almost imperceptible presence around her abdomen was now most definitely
there and had required yet another shopping trip
exclusively for maternity wear. Roman thought she
might have only a few more weeks before being vis-
ibly pregnant, provided she wore very loose cloth-

ing. And part of him couldn't wait until the moment he could see it, the constant proof that his wife was carrying his child.

They'd had the second scan—the first for them both together—and the scariest. But the tests came back clear and they had both heaved an emotional breath, reached for each other in that moment, seeking and finding support, and Roman felt another stone in the wall around his heart break loose.

But as the stones fell, fear came with it, slipping through the cracks. Insidious whispers and thoughts he fought valiantly to keep from his wife. His innocent wife, who had been punished enough for his actions. She had tried to keep her own disappointment at failing to secure the client from him, but he had not missed the worried phone calls to her business partner, Célia. That Ella sought to protect *him* from the responsibility of it ate at him. He might have lived his whole life walking his path of vengeance alone, but he no longer felt like the Great Wolf—a name he had once delighted in.

He had found himself a pack, and Dorcas had taken to fiercely protecting Ella, following her everywhere she went, resting her head on her lap when Ella would sit, almost as if guarding their child.

Her words from the night of the ballet performance had run through his head as if on a loop, in time with his breathing and heartbeat. Her assurance that he could be enough, that he could be more than he had been. For her. With her. It had been a seductive call and it had somehow morphed into being his want and need.

He realised he wanted to embrace all the things that he had hidden from for so long. That he wanted a future with her, not just because of their child, but because of her. In the days since he had spoken to her of his mother, other memories had surfaced. Fractured moments of his mother laughing, the feel of her hand on his cheek, the way she had swept back the hair from his forehead and placed a kiss there. For years he'd only remembered the sadness, and now he saw that his mother had given him so much more. And, rather than pushing the memories back down as he had as a young man—as he'd needed to—or quickly refocusing his mind on some damned pursuit of vengeance, he took the time to remember, to hold them up and inspect them, feel them and embrace them. And it had caused a painfully sweet yearning for the love he'd forgotten.

None of which would have happened without his wife's belief that there was something worth saving within him, something worth preserving there for their future. For their child's future. His mother had once made him feel like that and now Ella was making him feel the same way.

And he wanted, *needed*, to give her something back, but felt it had to be perfect, that he had to do everything in his power to give her what she so greatly deserved.

Which was why, he justified to himself, he had made the call. Loukas Liordis was a Greek billionaire with a bad-boy reputation to match. And Roman, after a particularly intense drinking session in his New York club three years before, knew Loukas needed to redeem that reputation. It was that which made him the perfect client for Ella and Célia. Loukas had agreed to keep his involvement a secret, more than happy if it would lead to the redemption of his reputation, and promised to find a way to reach out to Ella through official channels.

But as the days wore on, without any word from Ella about a surprise new business contact, Roman began to regret his impulsive decision.

Instinctively, he knew that Ella would see it as an act of deceit, of going behind her back in precisely the way she had forbidden. Even in his attempts to make things right, to do and be better, he was starting from an act of betrayal. He'd even begun to hope that Loukas would have forgotten, would somehow have changed his mind.

Until he heard the most unlikely scream of delight from his wife and cursed inwardly, because he knew. All his hopes had been in vain. Because whether Loukas revealed his involvement or not, he knew that Ella would find out. And she would never forgive him.

Better to ask forgiveness than permission, his inner voice whispered seductively, even though something in his chest cried foul.

Ella came running down the steps, pausing midway when she saw him in the grand hallway of their house in France. The pure joy shining from her eyes and lighting her features made his heart drop, even as a smile pulled at his lips.

'Can we go to Fiji?'

'What?' he replied, not quite expecting her request.

'Fiji—can we go? Célia can't, and I...we might have a client, and I've never been and it would be—'

'Of course,' he said, willing in that moment to give his wife anything...anything but the honesty she had made him swear to.

'Are you sure you don't mind? I know that you must be busy with Kolikov Holdings and your own business.'

With yet another whip lashing against his conscience, Roman smiled through the self-recrimination. 'When are we going?'

She looked uncertain for the first time. 'Tomorrow?'

He laughed at this, not at Ella's uncertainty but the speed with which his future could come crashing down upon him. The impending moment when his wife would realise that he would not, could not, be what she needed him to be. The moment she would realise that he was so irretrievably damaged by his past that he could not hope for his future.

'Of course, Ella. Whatever you wish.'

Because he could at least give her this. He could ensure her future was secure, even if his was not.

Viti Yalo was a private island in the South Pacific that only allowed seventy visitors at any one point. As the private jet approached the small landing strip Ella peered at glimpses of paradise through the small round window. Turquoise sea and slashes of white sand bordered lush green patches peppered with tiny brown rooftops and the little square tiles of infinity pools that seemed unnecessary when next to the beautiful South Pacific Ocean.

It was a patchwork quilt of the dreams of the rich and famous—and suddenly Ella felt neither rich enough nor famous enough to be here. But her husband descended the small steps of the aircraft, covered the short distance towards the sleek black limousine waiting for them and barely spared a glance for the uniformed driver holding the door open for him as if he did this kind of thing every day.

She marvelled at the inherent power and authority of her husband. Wished and wanted to borrow it for herself. Because despite the brave face she had worn since Ivan had turned them down Ella had begun to fear that, although he had given the reason as her husband, it was her business plan that was the problem. It was a fear she had kept to herself, not wanting to betray Célia's confidence any further.

She had been relieved when Roman had agreed to her request that they arrive two days prior to the meeting with Loukas Liordis, so that she could prepare the pitch and the specifics and details and all the other minutiae that was in all likelihood unnecessary. But she would be prepared this time. Not willing to let herself, her business or Célia down. And, in some small way, determined to prove herself to her husband too.

But all Ella's internal musings were cut short when they arrived at the one-storey dwelling where they were staying. At each corner of the main house sat triangular turrets of a sort, bamboo thatching topping the roof of the building that sat squat and wide, clinging to the edge of the ocean. Stone arches indicated several rooms with windows that looked out across the water, a small pathway at the side of the house leading towards a long stretch of white sandy beach, dotted with palm trees. A somewhat improbable glass-encased pool sat to the left of the house and the sweep of the bay ensured complete privacy from any other dwelling nearby.

'I've changed my mind,' she said, laughing at the look of concern—almost horror—that passed across Roman's features. 'I don't want to live in France any more. My grandmother will be fine. Let's just move here!' she cried in delight as she ran to the doorway of the house, desperate to see what treasures she could find inside.

Every single room had large windows revealing the incredible view of the ocean. The two rooms bracketing either end of the house simply opened out onto the elements. Large hurricane lamps swinging gently in the breeze hung from the ceiling and swayed before large sprawling round benches that could easily have been the most exquisite beds covered in cushions and draped in throws that had her imagining a sunset with her husband beside her and... She broke off that train of thought as her cheeks heated and her pulse began to thump.

It was a luxurious fantasy, magical in the sheer opulence of it all. In the central living area, on the table had been placed a large vase of gloriously bright crimson flowers, beautiful in their bloom. A bottle of champagne, glistening with condensation, sat in a bucket beside two glasses, and a bowl of chocolate-tipped strawberries nestled on ice cubes. And that barely even began the welcome package the island had left for them.

As she moved through every room she saw signs of small gifts and touches that made her feel like a princess. Rose petals on the floor of the most beautiful bedroom she'd ever seen, swathes of richly patterned silk wraps for her to keep with 'our compliments'. Local artisanal paintings hung on the pure white walls, adding splashes of colours Ella would never have imagined liking, spreading joy through her, covering over her fears and concerns about the upcoming meeting—and suddenly she wished they were there just for them.

Everywhere she looked, the hypnotic horizon of the ocean was displayed in the distance and she thought that she never wanted to leave.

Roman found her where she had dropped herself onto the plush sofa, gazing at her as if searching for approval. She smiled. 'I think I could lower myself to spend a few days here,' she said mockingly.

'Very gracious of you,' he replied and she loved the teasing tone in his voice, so different from the husband who had seemed pressed down under an invisible weight she couldn't fathom since the night at the ballet.

'We have reservations at the restaurant...' and Ella couldn't help but feel a little crestfallen at the idea of leaving this beautiful place, even in all likelihood for an equally beautiful place, but she didn't want to share this. Share Roman. She wanted to tuck herself into this magical bubble and never leave. 'But I'm sure we could ask them to bring the food here.'

It was startling how easily he could read her. She'd never thought herself that expressive, but Roman seemed to know, to sense what she was thinking—sometimes even before she did.

'This is going to be impossible,' she almost wailed, once again mockingly. 'How am I supposed to focus on a business proposal with all this...?' She gestured around her, searching for a word that would express even an ounce of the beauty she was staring at. But for once she wasn't looking at the ocean, or the rooms, or the beautiful things contained within. She was looking at her husband. A husband who did not seem hungry for food in that moment.

Roman couldn't, wouldn't, stop the smile lifting his lips at his wife's insincere complaints. He had wanted to give her this—to give her everything and more.

'First, we eat. And during our meal you can practise your pitch as much and as many times as you need. But after...that time is for us,' he promised.

'Nope. Don't need to. I know it by heart. Let's just skip to the "us" time,' she said, reaching for him, pulling him towards her.

He placed a kiss on her lips, chaste and sweeter for it, and pulled away. 'I am simply making sure that you go into the meeting feeling completely prepared,' he gently whispered, refusing to be responsible for any further damage to her career.

Her large round eyes, matching the colour of the turquoise sea behind her, flickered with understanding, seeming to sense his guilt, and she reluctantly agreed.

Over a first course of filo pastry wrapped scallops in a creamy leek sauce, finished with fresh figs, Ella outlined the strategies of placing Loukas's business with handpicked charities within Greece and across the globe. Through the second course of sous-vide lobster with a mango, avocado, red onion and lettuce salad, Ella described how she and Célia would ensure each event and investment would be carefully curated by them, all communication running through them in order to filter only information of the utmost importance to him directly, reducing the tax on his precious time. And over a dessert of gingerbread cannoli, kirsch mousse and cinnamon ice cream, she delivered the financial incentives for offsetting some of his extraordinary wealth against global tax breaks and outlined how the positive impact of the publicity garnered would be immeasurable.

By the time coffee was served, Roman was halfway to demanding she drop all and any interaction with Liordis and muscling in as her first client himself. He was impressed. The vague gathering of thoughts she'd had when they had first met in France had been honed, stripped back and fine-tuned to the point of excellence. Ivan had been a fool. A fool that he was pleased his wife had not succeeded with. Liordis, he was sure, would not make the same mistake.

'And now,' she demanded, placing her knife and fork together on the plate, 'can we please—pretty please—get to the "us" time?'

Yes, everything in Roman roared. Whatever she wanted, while she still wanted it, he would give.

Two days later Ella swept into the restaurant she and Roman had still not visited. She felt…powerful. Powerful and sensual and confident. The soft white linen shift reaching to her thighs and a deceptively comfortable pair of palazzo trousers in a beautiful rust colour were both elegant and practical. Because, Ella realised, this would be the last business meeting that she could have while still disguising her pregnancy.

She was not naïve—she knew that her pregnancy could affect the way some potential clients viewed her and her future involvement in any deal she would secure. But both she and Célia had already decided that they would not be the clientele they would wish to attract. Roman had reassured her that it was unlikely to worry Liordis and she trusted him. Nothing would dim the excitement she felt thrumming through her veins. It was almost an echo of the sensual delight her husband had driven her to on the two preceding evenings as they'd watched the sun descend over the South Pacific Ocean, as their cries of pleasure mingled with those of exotic birds and the unconscious rhythm of their bodies followed the gentle sweep of waves moving back and forth over the beach below.

Ella would not have needed the careful guidance of the head waiter to direct her to Loukas Liordis. The man sat at a table on the decking, separated from the rest of the customers inside the restaurant, who were unable or unwilling to prevent the curious glances they cast his way. Although there were a few other tables dotted around the sweeping decking,

Ella knew that they would have the space entirely to themselves so that no one would be able to eavesdrop on their conversation. She had ensured as much.

She took the short walk winding between the other diners to look at the man she hoped would be her and Célia's first client. With his view secured on the horizon, she could take her fill. He was very attractive—Ella could see how he had earned his wicked reputation—and was even mildly surprised not to feel something within her pull towards his impressive aura. But a red ribbon had formed around her feelings for her husband, one that would never be severed by anyone other than Roman.

Even sitting, she could tell he was tall. Low brows lay heavily over deceptively slumberous eyes and the tawny hair, stylishly chaotic, almost roguish in its refusal to adhere to neatness, was a surprise to someone who expected to see darker features. His full lips drew into a large smile as he stood upon seeing her and graciously met her with a kiss to each cheek.

'Ella,' he said, and the informality of using her first name, the intimacy it invited, would probably have made another woman swoon. The heat of his hand at her arm and the smell of his cologne, all appealing, yet Ella found herself immune—as if her body craved only one touch, one scent, one person.

'Mr Liordis,' she replied.

'Loukas, please,' he said, charmingly, refusing to return to his seat until she had taken her own.

They ordered their drinks, his gaze not once wavering from her face as she requested a tonic water, as if he didn't need to look for confirmation of her situation. Although no expression passed over his features, she realised in an instant that it wouldn't do to underestimate this man, despite his lazy demeanour. Whether he realised her pregnancy or not, he had the grace not to allude to it.

'You are here with your husband?' he asked.

'Yes,' she said, unable to keep the smile from her face.

'Ah, then I will not keep you from him for long, for this place is a paradise for lovers.'

Loukas proceeded to explain that he'd been looking for a charity to put his energies into for some time, but had been hampered by his reputation. He was charming, self-deprecating, but with a fierce intelligence she recognised from her husband. She read between the lines and a little thread of excitement curled through her as she realised that he needed them as much as they needed him.

But, for all his practised charm, Ella found herself longing for the dark edges and plain speaking of her husband, figuring them somehow more real than the careless façade Loukas was presenting.

The meeting was going well. Really well. He had listened with a focus that simmered beneath the languorous gaze, had questioned a surprising amount of the finer details, yet Ella had risen to each one—

and she could tell that he was impressed. Impressed and tempted. However, she could feel the 'but' on the horizon and she began to feel the first prickling of concern.

'This is a very strong business plan, Ella. Your anticipation of many of my concerns has been impressive, and I really would like to look into this further.'

'But?' she asked with a smile to take the sting out of her fear.

'But I do have one concern. I'm not quite sure yet that your company is financially viable enough to do what I need you to do for me.'

'I assure you that we are.'

He grimaced as he shook his head, clearly not convinced, but also clearly not refusing them outright. 'If you can show me that there is more capital, say between four or five million, then I would readily sign the papers. But without it…' He trailed off and shrugged apologetically.

As Ella's stomach dropped, her mind furiously spun, filtering through her private bank accounts, calling to mind Célia's own investments. There was one option, her only option. But would she take it?

'Would you be willing to give me two days?'

'Of course,' he replied. 'I do believe in your company and what you are offering and would very much relish the opportunity to work with you and your clients. Get in touch when you're ready and we'll talk.'

* * *

Roman had been pacing almost since the moment Ella had left to meet Liordis. Whether because of the effect he had had on her last client meeting or that he had come to see just how much this meant to Ella, this meeting had eclipsed even his own business interests in importance.

And while he had been the one to bring Loukas to the table, still as yet undiscovered by his wife, he had not been assured of the outcome. In what felt like a matter of minutes Ella returned, and he was shocked to find, when he checked his watch, that nearly two hours had gone by.

He realised immediately that something was wrong. The way she looked not at him but at the horizon, her mind clearly whirring away rather than relishing the joy of success. It ate at him, and even the knowledge that he should wait until she was ready couldn't prevent the question falling from his lips.

'What happened?'

'He… Loukas does want to sign with us…'

'But?'

She let loose a gentle, not quite bitter half-laugh at something he couldn't fathom.

'He doesn't think we have the capital to do what we say we can.'

'He's wrong,' Roman declared with a finality that surprised them both.

'Maybe…maybe not. He made some suggestions that were surprisingly astute—'

'Given his reputation?'

'Yes. It would most definitely not do to underestimate him. But I can't deny that those suggestions might stretch us, given our current finances.'

'Yes, but trying to arrange for more capital could stretch you further,' Roman responded, quickly seeing to the heart of her concern.

'Maybe. But…' She turned to him then, her hands rolling over each other before her, an unusually insecure gesture from his wife. 'But if I were to sell you my shares in Kolikov Holdings—'

'No.' Roman's quick, determined response surprised them both.

'Roman,' she chided. 'Will you hear me out?'

'I don't need to.'

'Roman,' she tried again, and he realised that she just couldn't see it. Couldn't see how giving him her shares, how handing control over to him would tempt him. Would give him the power to take it all away. She would hand over the very thing that kept him on a leash. And instinctively he knew. He knew that should she lose that hold, should she lose the last bargaining chip she had with him, it would destroy everything. Because he would be unable to resist putting those shares to the very use that she would not want. No matter how much she had come to mean to him, no matter how much he wanted to be more…he simply wasn't capable of it. He couldn't change. He had needed to be a monster to fight Vladimir and he was still that same monster. His…feelings for her hadn't changed that. And if he did use the shares to achieve what he wanted, the cost to Ella would be devastating. Her pain and the shock of a second betrayal…it would be too much for her to bear.

'Firstly,' he tried, desperately and silently needing her to understand, 'I don't want you to overstretch your company at such an early stage in its development. At the moment you are risking a great deal. If I say yes, you would risk even more. And secondly, we haven't actually done a market share price, so I couldn't honestly say that you'd get a fair price.'

'I believe in what Célia and I are doing. I believe in this company and know, *know*, it will work. And I don't need a market price, I need a fair one. And I trust you to be fair. I don't need more. I just need enough. And I think five million is a fair and appropriate price. It's enough to inject some of it into the company and still have a cushion that allows for some wiggle room.'

'Please think about this.' He was almost begging. Never before had he felt that sense of a precipice before him.

'Roman, honestly, I don't need to. I know that this will work, I know that this is what I need. Please, would you buy the shares from me?'

And his earlier promise came back to haunt him.

That he would give her anything she wanted, while she wanted it from him. Only this time, giving Ella what she wanted…would cost him everything.

Within two days the money had come through from the sale of her shares to Roman, Loukas had happily signed the paperwork, becoming their first client, and Ella was almost bursting with joy. She knew that she had put all of her eggs in one basket, but it was a basket that she and Roman shared. She was investing not only in herself, but them.

Roman was still out wrapping up things with the bank and Kolikov Holdings as Ella watched the sun begin its descent into the South Pacific Ocean. It felt so strange to have the night sky begin to glow about three hours earlier than France, adding to the feeling of a stolen moment outside of time. Ella shivered a little, remembering the last time she had felt like this—before her marriage to Roman. A time that she had felt just belonged to them.

But this was different, she told herself. This was their second chance. How it should have been all along. With a hand soothing over the gentle bump of her abdomen, Ella marvelled at just how much had changed since she had met him that day in the woods near her grandmother's cottage. In some ways, everything she had wanted back then had come to pass. Her marriage to Roman, her business, even their child, she acknowledged.

She might not have liked how they'd got here, but she couldn't wish it away. Had it not been like that, she might never have got to know the real Roman. Neither the one who had appeared perfect nor the one who had appeared monstrous had been the man she had come to…had come to…

Love.

With a surety that shocked her, the knowledge raced along her veins, fizzing in her blood and lighting something like pure joy within her. She did love him. She loved the man who would do anything to protect their child, the man who had confessed the deep pain hidden beneath his quest for vengeance, the one who still slept lightly in the hope that his mother would one day come and wake him and dance for him in the moonlight. The man who brought her exquisite pleasure and the man who had given her the ability to secure the business she and Célia had worked so hard for.

Energy raced through her body and she wanted to move, to dance, to take this moment and embrace the sheer happiness of it, having reached such a low shortly after her marriage. She picked up her phone and found a song on her music list, one that would perfectly echo everything she feared she might never capture in words.

As the song began the notes swept around her, filling the space and echoing in her heart, asking that she feel love. And she did. Paying no heed to the thought

that someone could come upon her, dancing around
the beautiful living space, with the most incredible
backdrop, Ella danced and danced and danced, an
almost intoxicating high running through her veins.

She performed another twirl, the layers of her
skirts spinning out from her waist, making her feel
like a child again, which was perhaps why she didn't
see Roman at first. Didn't see the look on his face
that might have stopped her in her tracks had she not
been so caught up in her joy.

Roman knew she hadn't seen him yet, and was thankful for it. Because it gave him time. Time to adjust
to the fact that, as she spun round the room, he saw
his mother. Ella's movements were not the elegant
sweeps his mother had made beneath the night sky.
Her arms didn't extend and reach out for something
intangible, as if the gesture would never end, never
stop reaching. Because, he realised, Ella believed she
had already found what she was looking for.

The happiness and joy he could almost see vibrating on the air about her, as she moved in time with
the song that taunted him, cut him off at the knees.

She turned to him then, eyes seas of sparkles that
would rival the night sky, and he knew. He didn't
want to, almost asked her not to say what she clearly
wanted to say. But his words wouldn't come, while
hers poured from her lips like raindrops.

'I'm so happy,' she said, almost strangely apologetic, or embarrassed. But those feelings were apparently put aside or pushed down as he watched her transform into someone assured, confident, someone owning her own sense of self. It was like watching a flower unfurl to bask in everything the sun could give.

'I couldn't have done it without you,' she said as she closed the distance between them. A distance that he wanted, needed, coward that he was. He wanted to explain that she was wrong. He wanted to ask her what she thought she might have been able to do had he not nearly destroyed her by seeking her as his tool for revenge. In a heartbeat, all the times he had seen her question herself because of him, doubt herself because of him, doubt those around her... Because of *him*, came to his mind.

'I love you,' she said. He didn't hear the words above the roaring in his ears but he saw them on her lips, felt them against his skin.

He kissed her then because he couldn't think of what to say, couldn't really begin to understand why her simple declaration could have scared him so much. But one thing he could imagine was the hurt and pain and devastation she would feel when she realised what he was about to do to Vladimir's company.

So he kissed her, stopping all words, all thoughts, all doubts and fears, as if this were the last time he would ever kiss his wife.

CHAPTER TEN

And the wolf gnashed his teeth and snarled,
hissed and bit and growled. It was his nature.
It was all he knew.
    The Truth About Little Red Riding Hood
         —Roz Fayrer

SHE HAD BEEN the root of her own downfall, Roman told himself as he marched through the offices of Kolikov Holdings in Moscow. The moment she had sold her shares to him, no matter how much she clearly felt that she had changed, had proved that she was just as innocent and naïve as she had been when he had met her over a year ago in France.

Yes, there was more there—a drive, a deeper complexity, a confidence and self-assurance that almost awed him. Almost. But she was still the same Ella who had agreed to marry a man after only one month of knowing him. And, like her, Roman was still the same as he had been when they had met. A man out for vengeance at any cost.

Ever since she'd let loose those three little words…

Too wrapped up in her thoughts and too busy since, Ella had absolutely no idea of the effect they'd had on Roman. They had haunted his dreams and sliced through his waking hours. The only other person to say such a thing to him had been cruelly torn from him without Roman being able to prevent it.

For so long he had been sure. Certain that his path of vengeance was just. For so long he had lived by the promise he'd made his mother on her deathbed. That Vladimir would be punished, that the company he'd loved more than his own child would be destroyed.

But Ella had made him want. Want things to be different, for *him* to be different. And he realised that for a few months he'd been living more of a lie than any he'd ever told. Because he'd lied to himself. Told himself that he could have things he didn't deserve. Could feel things that his closed off, damaged heart would never be capable of. That he could, in some impossible way, compensate for the truly awful things he had done to Ella.

And it had lasted until she'd asked him to buy her shares. Until she'd given him the final tool to complete the journey he had started almost eighteen years before. And he'd known. Known that he could not, would not refuse to use it.

Because if he put aside his plans now, if he changed his mind, then it would mean that every single thing he'd planned, done, right down to marrying Ella in the first place…it would have all been for nothing. And that was impossible. All the things he'd given up, all of the softer parts of him he'd sacrificed in order to exact revenge against Vladimir, all of the things that Ella deserved were gone.

Roman could not have, or *be,* both. He couldn't love her and not pay the price of his own actions. He couldn't love her and not acknowledge that he was more dangerous to his wife and child than any other threat they could face. So the only thing left to him was to burn it all down to the ground. Every last piece of Vladimir's company—and his marriage along with it.

Because that was the only way to protect Ella and their child, to ensure that his decisions and actions didn't hurt them beyond repair. To ensure that the damage done to his soul by so many years of vengeance didn't poison their innocence. The greatest act of love he could show either of them was to walk away.

He paused just outside the doorway to the boardroom, filled with the sycophantic men and women who had bolstered his grandfather's ego, who had come to represent all that had been inflicted on his mother. In that moment he felt hatred course through his veins. A hatred that *had* to be more powerful than anything else in him if he was to finally get what he'd wanted. A hatred he needed if he was to overcome the desire to turn back. To seek what he did not deserve. To throw himself at Ella's feet and beg for forgiveness. With gritted teeth, he hung on to his anger like a drowning man, walked through the doorway and came to a halt at the head of the table.

'Ladies and gentlemen, I have a proposition for you. One that you would be inconceivably stupid not to accept...'

Célia's laughter rained over Ella, who had not been able to stop smiling since Fiji. They had celebrated the success of securing their first client with a lovely long lunch—Célia sipping on champagne and Ella on ginger and elderflower *pressé*.

She leaned a shoulder against Célia's as they stood at the large iron-work windows of their beautiful new office that looked out over Paris. The nineteenth-century building had needed extensive work to make it a space suitable for their needs, but Célia had risen to the challenge. Ella loved the exposed brickwork and open space of the central offices, settling beneath steel girders that gave it a heady sense of both history and modernity, melded in the way in which they both wanted their business to bring together charities and businesses in order to help those who most needed it.

'You've done such a great job here, Célia.'

'And you've done such a great job with the clients,' Célia replied, smiling and leaning back into Ella.

Ella couldn't, wouldn't, disguise the little squeal

of delight, the little jump of joy, nor the smile when she caught Célia rolling her eyes.

'Are you sure you didn't have a drink at lunch?'

'Not a drop.'

'Then you're high on hormones and happy ever afters,' Célia almost groaned.

'I'm high on success,' Ella said, pulling on Célia's arm. 'After Loukas, I thought we might have some client interest, but three secured, and four more speculative?' Ella let out another childlike exclamation of glee before sweeping a hand over the now definitely visible bump beneath her loose shirt.

Célia's eyes caught the gesture, and Ella felt just a little bit of guilt. 'Are you sure you're going to be okay taking on the client-facing work while I'm…'

'On maternity leave?' Célia smiled. 'I will be. I *have* to be,' she concluded somewhat ruefully. Ella knew how much Célia disliked being the centre of attention, had witnessed more than once the panic that would descend over her shy friend.

'Please know that you can call me at any time.'

'Hmm, except when you're breastfeeding, changing nappies or gazing adoringly at your husband and child,' Célia joked then rolled her eyes again when Ella descended into another happy squeal. 'You're incorrigible! I still have to get the figures to the accountants by end of play today, and—'

'And, and, and. I know. Off you go. I'm just going to sit here for a moment and admire all the amazing work you've done getting the offices in such beautiful shape before I head back to Puycalvel.'

Ella sank into the swivel chair and swept back around to face the desk that looked out onto the offices, her heart leaping at the sight of Roman striding across the parquet flooring as if nothing else existed other than her. He was so focused that he clearly hadn't even seen Célia's awkwardly raised hand in greeting, but any slight Ella might have felt on her friend's behalf was buried under the happiness she felt at his unexpected visit.

She had risen and crossed the length of her new office by the time he had reached the doorway. She couldn't help but reach for the lapels on his jacket to pull him closer to her, smiling at the sense of decorum he had in her office space, while she had none. She went to kiss her husband, but he held back.

Finally looking at him closely, she could see signs of strain at the corners of his eyes and mouth, the clench of his jaw.

'Is everything okay?'

His reply was a slight inclination of his head—one that suggested, maybe not so much.

'Come. I have something to discuss.'

Frowning and knowing better than to push Roman until he was ready, she picked up her large cream leather handbag and followed him from the office.

He led her out onto the Parisian street, where a

limousine was waiting and whisked them a short distance before stopping.

'Where are we—?'

As she exited the limousine, Roman holding the door to the vehicle open for her, she stepped out onto a street in front of Comte Croix, a three Michelin starred restaurant that reputedly took bookings half a year in advance. For a moment she was speechless—she had always wanted to come here—and Ella warned herself not to inform him of her recent lunch with Célia. Of course, now that she was eating for two, she determined to enjoy every single minute of the treat Roman had organised for her.

As they walked through the two majestic wrought-iron gates into the restaurant, Ella was distracted from her brooding husband for a moment by the incredible French-English classical style of the establishment. Louis XIV furniture greeted them as they passed large regency mirrors and the gold and grey colours of the room soothed nerves Ella didn't realise she had. It was only as they reached the main seating area that she realised they were the only people in the whole restaurant.

She looked up, confused, at Roman.

'We have the place to ourselves.'

She laid a hand on his arm as if to convey some sense of the awe that she was feeling in that moment, the sheer magnitude of his power and wealth on full display. If she thought it odd that he was the

one who directed her to a table nestled within a sea
of others, each covered in crisp white tablecloths and
ready to serve no other customer, she didn't think on
it too much. At that moment, she was staring up at
her husband with moon-eyed love and couldn't help
but laugh at the situation.

'I can't work out whether this is incredibly roman-
tic or incredibly unnecessary,' she said, her stomach
turning slightly under the still firm set of Roman's
features.

'I have a few things I want to discuss,' he said,
pulling two thick envelopes from the inside of his
jacket and placing them before her on the table. He
pushed one closer towards her with his forefinger. 'I
need your signature on some documentation.'

Ella, trying to shake off the feeling that something was terribly wrong, retrieved the envelope and
slipped out the paperwork.

'It is a trust fund for your child.'

As she scanned the documents, the sheer amount
that Roman had secured in trust for their child
shocked her enough not to realise the oddly chosen
words from her husband.

'It secures that amount in place until their twenty-
fifth birthday—or their marriage, whichever comes
first. Until then, you will be the sole trustee.'

She came to the last page, where a yellow plastic
tab pointed to a line next to the one Roman had already signed. The tab was oddly horrible and prac-

tical against the smooth beauty of the table and their surroundings. She couldn't quite tell why she was oddly resentful of its presence, but she was.

Roman produced a pen and passed it to her, the thick silver barrel weighty in her small hand, but still warm from where it had sat nestled next to Roman's body inside his jacket.

As she signed the papers her hand shook just a little and Ella was unsure as to why.

Still, when she had finished, she placed the pen on the tablecloth. 'Done,' she said, struggling for a smile, struggling with a strange sense of something she couldn't quite grasp.

'And these,' he said, pushing the other envelope towards her in a similar fashion as before, as if the contents were somehow disdainful to him, 'are divorce papers.'

She had started to pull the papers from the envelope, started to scan the tight neat rows of printed words, with legal headings topping the pages, found the page with another horrible yellow tab pointing to where another signature from Roman had been scrawled, had almost put pen to paper, when his words finally registered and the thick sheaf dropped onto the table.

'What?' she demanded, shaking her head as if she could deny his words, deny the dawning realisation spreading through her body as if to protect her heart for as long as possible.

Roman leaned back in his chair, as if already wanting to remove himself as much from her presence as possible.

'Four hours ago the shareholders of Kolikov Holdings agreed to begin the liquidation process.'

'But—'

'You're not a shareholder any more.'

A sharp inhale was about all Ella could manage.

'Roman, is this some kind of joke? Because it's not funny.'

'It's no joke. And you're right, it's not funny.'

'I don't understand.'

'I could see that the moment you asked me not to destroy Vladimir's company. And then later again, when you wanted to sell me your shares, even though I asked you to reconsider.'

Roman knew then that he was surely going to hell. Everything in him fought, raged, snarled against the words coming from his mouth, words that would eternally sever his connection to this incredible woman and his child. *His child.* But he had to. If not for Ella's sake, then for the sake of that very same child.

Many months ago, Ella had voiced her desire, her need for freedom. And Roman had realised that it might just be the only thing he could give her. And in order to do that, in order to really ensure that she was in no doubt about the need to have that freedom, that distance, he would have to make her hate him more than she had ever done before.

'You saw it when…when I asked you not to destroy the company? But that was… That was months ago, Roman. Have you planned this the whole time?' she asked, her voice thick with the tears he could see about to fall from her cornflower-blue eyes.

'Yes,' he lied. 'The whole time,' he said, unable to bear the sight of his wife so distraught any more. Instead, he focused his gaze over her shoulder, but was unable to avoid the images of Ella dancing in Fiji, seeing her cry her pleasure the night they'd shared at the gazebo, seeing the way she had looked at him the night they had conceived their child, with wonder and awe and—even then—the beginnings of a foolish love.

'I was the one who called Loukas,' he said, knowing that this would lay bare the true darkness within him.

'You…what? I don't… I thought…'

'You thought wrong. I have known Liordis for nearly four years. Knew that he'd been looking for something that would redeem him in the eyes of the world. He was perfect for what I needed of him, and what you wanted of him.'

'And you got him to demand the money that I could only achieve by selling my shares.'

It was a statement. Not a question. And he was thankful for that, for it meant he didn't have to lie about that, he could simply let her assume the worst.

And somehow, even though that was his intention, it hurt. It hurt that she could so easily believe that of him—and he realised that painful bitter irony of his hurt. Because that was precisely why he was doing this. Because, for all her declaration of love, of trust, she couldn't really love him or trust him. He had done far too much damage before they'd even had a chance at something more. He knew that. And far better for it to end now than later. Than after he had let down his guard, after he had allowed himself to fall...

He cut off that thought with a sharp slashing movement of his hand, which Ella seemed to interpret as confirmation of her supposition.

'Once you sold me your shares I was finally able to destroy Kolikov Holdings. And if there is any justice in this world then Vladimir is turning in his grave, knowing that I, not he, got the last laugh.'

'Laugh?' she demanded. '*Laugh?* You dare reduce my life and the life of our child to a *laugh*?'

She was shivering now, but with anger, with fury. And it incited his own.

'*Nyet*. No. No, I would not.'

'I loved you.'

'Then it can't have been that great a love if it is already gone.'

Nausea swelled in her stomach, her hand sweeping to soothe, to calm the erratic kicks she could feel there as if even their child was reeling with horror at her husband's...her... *Roman's* actions.

She thought then that she might have seen him flinch, might have seen the tightening of his jaw and an echo of the pain that she felt rising within her, but knew she was wrong. Because this man...wasn't capable of such a feeling. Gone was her fiancé, who had indulged her every whim, gone was the husband who had confessed his pain, his hopes for the future, his passion and, she had once thought, a bourgeoning love, in his touches and kisses. This man was new— he had neither the smooth charm of the former nor the hot anger and heated passion of the latter. This was someone cold to her. Someone almost dead to her.

Her soft heart cried foul, desperately torn by the hope that he was lying. That her husband had not utterly manipulated her once again. He had arranged the meeting with Loukas to make her hand over her shares? That was a blow too low. That all the while she had been hoping for the future and he had still been held in the past, where vengeance and the need for destruction were his only focus.

'What kind of monster are you?'

'The kind your grandmother warned you about. The kind that would steal more than your innocence. A monster made in my grandfather's image. One who was only ever after the money I could get from Kolikov Holdings' liquidation—a small compensation for the life of my mother. One who would do whatever it took to get what I wanted. And who is letting you go now that I *have* what I want.'

Unaccountably, images from their time together rose in her mind. The first time she'd felt as if he were stalking her in the woods, the weight of the red cloak around her shoulders, the glimpse of him smiling at her joy in Fiji, the way he had looked at her when she had asked him to buy her shares, almost with fear, as if he didn't want her to do that. There was a fervour in him now that she had never seen before. An almost wild determination, as if he were trying to convince her of something too much. Too hard. Money? He'd said it was about money?

She shook her head, hating the way her thoughts, even now, seemed to want to find the good in him. Wanted to find the truth in the lie. Only there were so many lies and so many versions of the truth, she simply didn't know any more.

So, instead of trying to find a way through, she tried for a way out. A way out of the only conclusion Roman was forcing them towards.

'Look me in the eye and tell me this was just about the shares. That all this time,' she demanded, 'it was about destroying the company. When you told me I would have to return to your side. When you told me our child needed its father. When you told me about the loss of your mother. When you lost yourself in my body, when you slept beside me all night long for the first time in years.'

'Puycalvel is still yours,' he said, as if completely ignoring her. 'Everything you came to this marriage with is still yours and yours alone—'

'Apart from the damn shares—'

Apart from my heart.

'For which you were paid generously.'

And for a moment she almost thought he'd been talking about her heart too.

'Have your lawyer look over the paperwork. If you would like to negotiate anything further, I will consider it—'

'How gracious of you,' she hissed, the ire taking over her heart and mind now flowing fully in her veins.

'And you will have full custody—'

'I would *never* let my child near you,' she spat.

'*Da*. It is probably for the best.'

She rose jerkily to her feet and stared in confusion at the arm Roman had offered to steady her. Confusion and disdain. She flinched away from it, knocking back the chair, and blindly wound through the tables that now seemed like obstacles to her. Her eyes brimming with tears, some escaping, falling to the floor from her cheeks, felt sore and her heart ached in a way she had never felt before.

It was so much worse than before. So much. Because she had really loved him. She'd been sure of it. Of him. He had asked her to trust him and she had. She had given herself to him and now felt oddly disconnected from everything. Her feelings, her confidence, herself.

His betrayal slashed through her a thousand times as she passed through the iron gates of the restaurant and out onto the bright sunlit Parisian street, as if emerging from some dark horror. She caught the frown of the waiting driver, the stares of passersby as they took in the sight of what must look like a hysterical woman on the verge of…on the verge of…

'Ella…'

She refused to turn to look at the man who had hurt her more than anyone else had ever done, she refused to see the stranger staring back at her with nothing more than cold dead eyes, uncaring and unfeeling. She didn't want to, couldn't, let that be the last thing she saw of him.

'Ella,' he said again, and she felt his hand on her arm, turning her back to him. She closed her eyes, hoping that the next words from his mouth would somehow contradict everything that had just happened. Would somehow explain what had just happened, and take it away. Beg for forgiveness, plead with her.

But when she opened her eyes, all she could see were the two envelopes in his other hand. He pressed them towards her as he looked over her head and told the driver to take her wherever she needed to go.

He finally turned his gaze on her, that cold, painful look in his eyes doing more to damage the fragile threads of any kind of hope in her heart, and said, 'It was all about the shares, the company, the money. All this time. From the very beginning to the very end, you were only a means to give me what I wanted.'

And as Ella fled from his grasp, into the back of the limousine, Roman realised that he had been wrong. He'd thought he'd known pain. He thought he'd survived the worst that life could throw at him. But he hadn't and he sure as hell didn't deserve to this time.

CHAPTER ELEVEN

Red Riding Hood had always thought her grandmother's tales were to teach her the difference between a hero and a villain or good and evil. But, she wondered, what if the only difference came down to who it was that told the story?

The Truth About Little Red Riding Hood
—Roz Fayrer

LOOKING OUT FROM the patio, down the sloping green garden towards the silvery thread of the lake winding across the border of her land, Ella saw the copper dome of the gazebo glinting in the morning sun. Since returning from Paris five days ago, she hadn't been back there.

And she hated Roman for that. It had been her favourite place in the grounds of her home. He'd promised that it would always be hers. But it didn't feel that way. Everywhere she turned, she saw him. She smelled him on the sheets that she had washed twice now, but it hadn't worked. It was as if his scent clung to the very air she breathed, and she had been driven outside by the memories that crashed through her relentlessly.

Ella hated the way her mind seemed incapable of creating walls around her heart and mind, instead opening her to everything she had experienced over the last few months, and before. All the different variations of the man she had married competing and contradicting everything she thought she knew.

Dorcas lifted her head as a flock of swallows soared above them on their long migration towards South Africa before the winter months, but didn't move from where she had taken up her almost constant guardianship. One eye on Ella at all times, and the other on the door as if waiting for her master to return.

She was glad Roman had left Dorcas with her. She didn't think she could have been here alone. Célia had offered to come and stay, but Ella had said no. There was too much going on with the company and too much breaking in her heart. She didn't want her friend to see her like this. It was something she needed to bear alone. Because she had done this to herself. She had been *so* stupid.

And, of all the things, that was what turned her stomach, fired the ache in her heart. He had fooled her once and the shame had been his. But this second time? And just as those insidious thoughts crept into her mind, her baby kicked and turned, and kicked again. As if reminding her that she'd had her reasons. That she'd wanted, so, so much, to give their child a better chance. A chance for something more than they had each had. And that she would never regret. But then the pain that Roman had taken that away from them began again.

Her first instinct had been to sever ties with Liordis. She was still very much struggling with the desire to do it now. She hated to think that he had been in on it with Roman. That he had been part of her manipulation. That he had professed his interest in her business not because of what they could do, or how good they were, but because he too was using her for her husband's ends. That Roman's interference had infected the one part of her life she felt completely her own had been devastating.

Célia had tried to reassure her, to insist that she would follow whatever Ella wanted to do with regards to the Greek billionaire. Let him go, keep him, whatever Ella wanted. No matter the effect on their business. But, despite how Ella felt personally about the man, she couldn't deny the damage that would be done should they choose to sever ties with their first client.

Yet that didn't mean she was willing to let it go.

As she dialled the contact number for Loukas, she took a fortifying breath. She could still do this. She was still the co-founder of the business. She was still capable—even if she had made terrible mistakes in the past, it didn't mean she would carry on that way. No. Unlike the men in her life, she would refuse to make decisions about her business for personal reasons.

'*Naí?*'

'Mr Liordis? It's Ella Riding.'

'Mrs Black?'

She flinched and was glad he wasn't there to see it. Incensed that the man would dare to use her married name.

'Not for much longer.'

'Oh, I am sorry to hear that.'

She almost growled at the man's audacity. For surely he would have known the full extent of Roman's plans, once he had his hands on her shares. Ignoring the platitude, she pressed on. 'I have something I want to discuss with you.'

'All ears, *agápe mou*.'

'If we are to continue to do business together—'

'Wait… What?' Loukas's shocked voice interrupted.

'Let me finish, Mr Liordis,' she commanded. 'If we are to continue to do business together, then we need to place all our cards on the table.'

'Okay…' His voice was laden with suspicion.

'When we did our deal, I was not aware of your interaction with my husband.'

'I wouldn't call it an interaction as such,' he stated.

'No? Asking me to fund an extra five million euros was not an *"interaction as such"*?'

There was silence on the other end of the phone—at being caught out? she wondered.

'Look, Mrs... Ella, I'm not quite sure what's going on here, but the only thing your...Roman...asked me to do was to take a business meeting. It was very much for both my and your benefit. I was the one who needed to be assured of your financial viability. Beyond that one request to listen to your proposal, there was no other interaction, other than a rather drunken night in his club in New York three years ago. I promise you, I do not mix business with pleasure. So, whatever you *think* passed between us, you are mistaken.'

He seemed to give her the time to take that in, but whatever pause he had left her was not enough.

'Now, I would still like to continue to work together very much and will happily put this down to a misunderstanding. But if you plan to sever ties with me, then I need to know now. I have other things riding on this, and will not risk a single one of them.'

Part of Ella wanted to rail against the dark commanding tone she encountered now from a man who had been seen as more playboy than billionaire, but she couldn't. Because she was lost in her own confusion.

'No, Mr Liordis. That won't be necessary. My apologies.'

'Think nothing of it,' he said, his tone instantly turning back to his usual charm. 'I shall look forward to seeing you in two months at the first gala.'

Ella cancelled the call and the phone fell from slightly shaking hands. Liordis had no reason to lie. Well, that was not actually true. There had very much been a sense in his response that had strongly indicated how important their business deal was to him. But his surprise at the question about the money had seemed genuine.

More genuine in some ways than Roman had sounded when he had claimed it had all been about the money. Because Roman had never been obsessed with money and the keeping of it. No, instead, money seemed to be something he was barely even aware of.

She forced herself to think back to that day in the restaurant. The divorce papers. The trust fund. Now that had been an obscene amount of... Of...

She almost tripped over Dorcas, trying to get back into the kitchen where she had thrown both sets of papers the moment she had returned from Paris, not daring to look at them since.

She gave herself a paper cut trying to get into the envelope and pulled out the thick bundle, still with the sticky yellow tab affixed. Instead of turning to that page, she started with the first, scanning and flipping through the pages until somewhere about the fifth page she stopped.

Looking at the inconceivable number of millions on the page outlined by little black print, she didn't have to wonder long at where all that money must have come from. It could only have been the total amount of the sale of Kolikov Holdings, give or take an extra five million.

Her husband had lied to her. Again. She howled out loud in frustration. What on earth was he doing? Because if it wasn't about the money, if he had given it all in trust to their child, then what was it really about? He had pushed her away. Telling her the only thing that would make her leave. Now she remembered all the bits and pieces he'd shared with her about his childhood. The machinations of a truly awful grandparent, the insecurities of having foster parents who'd never really wanted him. Now she remembered how sincere he'd been about asking her to rethink the sale of her shares. He'd almost pleaded with her not to do it. Now she remembered how he had claimed to be a monster made in his grandfather's image. But he hadn't been. She'd seen him. The day he'd discovered he was going to be a father… the pain and desperation as he'd told her about his mother…the night he'd said that he could only hope to be the man she deserved to have by her side.

And she'd said, *'Trust me.'* She'd asked him to trust her to know that he *was* better. And she had been the one to break that trust. She had been the one, despite knowing that the man demanding a divorce didn't seem like her husband, didn't seem the man she'd fallen in love with, who had broken that trust.

Oh, God, she thought, a shaking hand to her mouth. For all her words of assurance, her apparent faith in him…she had believed the one lie he'd truly told her, the one that had fed her fears rather than her faith. And she'd done exactly what he'd expected her to do. Think the worst. To leave. Just like everyone else in his life had done.

Roman strode through the tables of the club in Russia, ignoring the slightly worried looks of his staff and oblivious to the gazes of his patrons. At first, after returning from Paris, he'd thought a numbness had descended, wrapping around him and protecting him. But then he'd realised. It wasn't numbness, but silence.

No more little tapping noises as Dorcas trotted behind him, her toes clipping along the hard wooden floors of his apartment. The little yips of joy or pleading whines, specifically designed to incite guilt or attention. No more warm weight on his thigh as she would lean into him. How on earth had a damned dog come to mean so much to the Great Wolf? he wondered ruefully.

And that had only been the beginning. Because as soon as he realised the absence of Dorcas, he knew it was masking the absence of *her*. Ella. His wife. Mother of his child. And suddenly he realised all the sounds that he would miss in the future. His child's first cry, first laugh, first word. He realised all the sounds he was already missing. His child's heartbeat. His wife's cry of pleasure, her gentle, teasing laugh, the sounds she made in her sleep unconsciously, the way her hand sounded as it swept towards him across the bedsheets.

All these noises that were consumed by the silence of his life. And even as a part of him wished he'd never met her, the other, the part of his heart still beating, still hoping, knew that he would be thankful for it for ever.

He knew what he'd done that day. Still held to the decision he'd made. Ella *was* better off without him. He had told her lies and she'd believed them. His mind taunted him with evil thoughts.

She never loved you. If she had, she wouldn't have believed you. She only ever loved the fiancé, the man you were not.

And he felt he deserved every single one of them. Because that questioning, that self-doubt, wasn't that what he'd done to her that first time? If he'd known what it had been like for her he never would have taken her innocence, never would have allowed her back into his life. Because this? This was pure hell.

So he took his punishment, knowing that he fully deserved it. Every single sharp twist of the knife, he would take a million times over because he had done worse to her.

And that was why, no matter how much he wanted to go to her, to beg her to take him back, to beg to spend each and every day seeking to make up for his awful actions, to be better, to do better, he would not. Because he would never be worthy of her.

He reached the corner of the bar, where a barman jumped to attention, knowing without Roman even having to ask for the bottle of vodka he'd appeared almost nightly to demand, before disappearing to his lair above the club.

The bottle appeared on the counter top and Roman swept it up and stalked towards the lift in the back corner of the room. But in his mind he was not holding the slippery condensation-covered chilled bottle, but the warm, slim crook of Ella's elbow, his palm heated despite the cool feel of the glass. As he swept his key card over the electronic plate he followed a ghost into the lift, unconsciously making space for the image of her with him.

Roman caught sight of the image of his reflection in the mirrored surface, barely meeting his own gaze. He grimly acknowledged that he looked like hell, the dark sweeps under his eyes speaking to the fact that he'd not been able to sleep fully through the night since he'd left her bed and, in all likelihood, wouldn't ever again.

The only thing that soothed the ache was that he'd provided for them both—Ella and their child. They would never want for anything. Certainly not for a husband or father who wasn't good enough, who wasn't worthy enough.

Was that what his mind had kept hidden from itself? he wondered. All these years and all that determination for vengeance. Had it hidden…this? These feelings and this fear he'd never voiced before he'd met Ella. Never needing to account for his actions or his behaviour to anyone before now.

He cursed and, rather than waiting to cross the distance of his living area to find a glass, unscrewed the lid of the bottle of *zubrowka* and raised it to his lips, anticipating the taste of the ice-cool alcohol on his tongue. But, before he could take a sip, he stopped, his hand hovering before his mouth, holding the bottle but not moving.

Ella sat on his sofa, encased in the red cape he had bought her, and he wondered whether he had finally lost all sense. Because surely his twisted mind had conjured her from his thoughts and memories. Surely she was not sitting there, her beautiful shapely legs crossed, her hands placed in her lap, her level gaze one that could easily be mistaken for serenity.

But he knew, the moment he took a breath, that she was real because her scent had filled the air of his apartment. A delicious taste of something almost like orange blossom, mint and memories.

Everything in him became alert, the hair at his nape raising slightly as his first fearful thought careened through him.

'The baby?'

'Is fine.'

He took a moment for her assurance to sink in,

to smooth out the erratic pulse of his heart, but it didn't work. He was still fired with adrenaline as if under threat, as if the ground was shifting beneath his feet. She looked incredible. Everything he'd ever wanted, right there, within touching distance, and he couldn't. He just couldn't.

'Then we have nothing to discuss,' he growled as he stalked past her to the kitchenette. 'You can let yourself out.'

'I could. But I won't.'

He hoped to high heaven that she didn't see the way his fingers shook as he reached for the glass he would have easily forgone just moments earlier. He felt a growl rising in the back of his throat, the need to lash out and release some, if not all, of this pent-up fury he felt rising in his chest. The fury of pain, of hurt, of loss.

All of it he swallowed as he forced himself to turn around and look towards his…well…if she was here with the divorce papers then he couldn't really call her his wife any more. Landing on that explanation for her appearance here in his apartment, a cold fist so fierce it burned struck his heart. That was it. That was why. It could only ever be that.

'You could have sent the papers to my lawyers. This,' he said with a sweep of his arm and the bottle he still held, 'is unnecessary.'

'On the contrary. I find it deeply necessary.'

'If there is something you want to contest—?'

'And if I wanted to contest the whole thing?'

Roman reared back as if slapped. 'I don't…'

'It's not often that you are lost for words, Roman.'

He stared at her, unsure what she was saying, unsure as to what was happening.

'What game are you playing?' he demanded.

She cocked her head to one side. 'The one you apparently decided we were playing.'

'Would you stop speaking in riddles!'

That his anger apparently caused her only to smile was deeply unsettling.

'I think that might be the first real and honest reaction to this whole damn thing since you took me to the restaurant. A tad ironic, but real at least.'

Roman ground his teeth together so hard he thought he might have heard something crack. For here she was again. The beautiful, proud, determined fury that he had met here six months ago. The woman who had seduced as much as been seduced. The woman who had become the mother of his child and keeper of his heart.

'You want my anger? Then get out,' he roared, even more horrified that his fury seemed to have exactly the opposite effect on Ella.

'But how am I supposed to witness your anger if I am gone? No, Roman. Surely better for me to be here and witness you in your full monstrosity, no?'

He wanted to hurl the bottle he still held against the wall beside him, and the only thing staying his hand was that somehow the glass might shatter and catch her. And when everything in him was screaming out to protect her, to keep her from *him*, that he could not do.

'What are you doing here? What do you want from me?' he demanded.

'I want to know why you lied.'

'Good God, Ella, everything I've ever said to you has been a lie.'

'Not everything. But certainly all that you said in the restaurant.'

He couldn't look at her. He had done that day, but it had taken everything in him and he no longer had the energy to fight. He knew that if she looked too hard, thought too much, she'd realise the truth. And he had to protect her from that.

'You are fooling yourself. Once again. So naïve.' He forced the cruel words through thin lips.

'But no longer innocent?'

'Have I not hurt you enough? Have I not proved to you how depraved and damaged I am?'

'I will not lie and tell you that. Because there have been too many lies between us and you have hurt me. And I'd not use *depraved*—that was your word—but damaged? Yes, you have been damaged, but not broken and not irretrievably so. I…' She paused, and he couldn't not look at her, couldn't not face whatever it was that she would say next. 'I owe you an apology.'

'Hell, Ella. What are you—?'

'I asked you to trust me. I asked you to trust me to know that you could be better. Trust that I knew that about you. And I let you down. Because at the first sign, the first suggestion that you might not be, I walked…ran even, not looking back. Not looking back enough to see the truth.'

He was shaking then. He was racked by it, the trembling that had started in his heart, spreading out through his body, and he felt the press of hot wet heat against the back of his eyelids. He couldn't do this. He couldn't…

'I told you that I loved you and I left.'

She was killing him. Tearing him apart with her words. All the things he had never wanted to face, never wanted to know or feel.

'I will not take *full* responsibility for that, because you did have a hand in that. But, for my part, I am sorry.'

He wanted to rush to her, drop to his knees and beg her forgiveness. Beg her to take him back, promise to do whatever it would take to make it up to her. Tell her that…that…he loved her more than life itself. But he couldn't. Not yet.

'Ella, please.' Roman no longer knew what he was asking for. For her to stop, or never stop.

'Tell me the truth,' she demanded and he owed her that much.

'I thought—*think*—that you deserve more. That you are owed more. After all that I have done, under the guise of vengeance… I simply don't know how to be. When you asked me to buy your shares, you didn't know what you were doing. Didn't know that it would give me the only possible chance of having what I had spent a lifetime wanting. I felt, believed, that if you did love me then you wouldn't ever have asked me to give that up. Kolikov Holdings was the last tie to my past, to my grandfather, to my mother's death…and I wanted, *needed*, it to be gone and you placed, in my hands, the ability to do so— and demanded that I didn't.

'Do you understand, Ella? Do you see? The promise I made to my mother on her deathbed, it was a promise that kept me alive, made me get up in the morning, drove me beyond anything else in this world to succeed and achieve the impossible. You made me promise not to do it, and I couldn't live up to that. I couldn't because my mother came first. That promise came first.'

For the first time since she had made him make that promise Ella realised the cost of it. Tears rose to her eyes at the position she had put him in, unwittingly. In her mind, the destruction of Kolikov Holdings was simply the embodiment of his betrayal—of Vladimir's betrayal—of *her*. She hadn't really thought what it had meant to him, what it had symbolised to *him*.

'Why didn't you tell me this? Why didn't you try

to explain?' she asked in a softer voice than the trembling she felt within her.

'And risk you leaving with my child?'

'A departure you specifically engineered only a few months later?' she couldn't help but interject.

'The few months it took me to realise just how much damage I could do to you. When I realised that I was too weak not to give in to the urge to destroy the last trace of Vladimir's hold on this world.'

Ella took a moment to think through his words, the pain and anguish clearly ringing within them. She had been so determined, so sure of her demand when she'd made it, she could see that she would have walked away. Her own pain and anger, the fierceness with which she'd thought she had been in the right.

Taking a breath, she made herself feel the intention of his words, to feel the truth of them.

'And now?' she asked.

'Now?' Roman seemed confused, as if in his mind there simply couldn't be a now.

'Yes. Now, how do you feel?'

'About Vladimir's company?' he asked.

'I don't care about the damn company and never want to hear its name again,' she cried. 'I want to know how you feel about me.'

She looked at him, watching his features closely as if they could give her some kind of hint or hope to what she believed he felt. He crossed the room to come before her, dropped to his knees and took her hands in his. 'There is nothing in this world more important to me. I love you with every single beat of my heart.'

Her own heart leapt, her hands shaking within the press of his.

'I would give anything to take back all the hurt I inflicted upon you, all the times you felt doubt, or questioned yourself because of me. I have had only a week of that myself and…' He broke off, shaking his head. 'I am truly sorry for it. And if you give me the chance I will spend each and every single day trying to make up for it. I will never, ever speak an untruth to you again. I will never make you doubt me, my love for you or our child. I will do whatever it takes, Ella. Because I love you. There is so much of it, there is no room for anything else. Not thoughts of vengeance, not the need to destroy. Just love. And all of it for you and our family.'

She was startled to feel the pad of his thumb sweep aside a tear she hadn't realised was there.

She reached for him then and pulled him towards her, delighting in the feel of his kiss, sweetened by her tears of joy.

'I love you,' she said between presses of her lips against his. 'So, so much,' she said. And that was the last thing he allowed her to say before sweeping her into his bedroom, closing the door and showing her how beautiful their lovemaking could, and would, be for the rest of their lives.

EPILOGUE

Cinderella, Snow White, Rapunzel...they each found their handsome prince. But Red Riding Hood found something so much more. She found her mate, her wolf...her pack. And in doing so she found herself.

The Truth About Little Red Riding Hood
—Roz Fayrer

ELLA STOOD IN the doorway to her daughter's room in Puycalvel watching the four-year-old spin slightly off-centred circles in her little pink leotard and ballet shoes, both of which were extremely cute but nothing compared to the full length pink, frothy, layered, sparkly tutu that Roman had produced for her just hours before.

It was completely over the top but Tatiana loved it and had refused to take it off, not even for bed, despite the warnings that she might damage it.

'I'm going to be the greatest ballerina ever,' she proclaimed between spins, 'but not as great as Grandma, because *no one* could be as good as Grandma.'

The sound of footsteps above on the staircase drew Ella's attention towards her husband, who had their second daughter in his arms as he made his way carefully down the steps. Not once had he ever betrayed his promise to keep her and their children safe, not once had he ever given her cause to feel anything but joy and love. Frustration sometimes and perhaps, even on occasion, a healthy dose of anger. But never sadness and never fear.

The moment his eyes found hers, the smile on his face brightened, his eyes widened with an awe she would never tire of as he took in her, once again, rounded form.

'We're going to have to stop at three, you know,' she warned in a voice still low from trying to settle her unruly daughter.

'Why?' he said, as if he would never tire of seeing her pregnant, of meeting the children they bore, of increasing the amount of love each time within their family. It seemed in almost never-ending supply.

'Because I want you to myself for a while,' she mock growled as he pressed a kiss to her cheek.

'You can have as much of me as you like, for however long you like. I am here, yours, always and for ever.'

'It's words like that that got me in this situation in the first place,' she moaned, her hands sweeping down around her bump. Their third child was due in a few months' time and neither parent could wait to meet the new addition to the family.

'I will keep saying them until they stop working,' her husband insisted.

'I want to see Auntie Célia and my cousins,' Tatiana announced, jumping up and down, despite the late hour.

'And we will, but tomorrow, sweetheart. Now, it's time for bed.'

'Nope. Not time for bed.'

'Yes, time for bed,' Roman chimed in, walking into his daughter's bedroom and sitting at the bottom of her bed. 'And you know what that means?'

'Story, story, story,' exclaimed Tatiana as Adeline clapped her hands together with as much coordination as an eighteen-month-old could manage.

'I believe it's your turn, wife,' Roman announced with a smile full of satisfaction and happiness. Ella believed that he loved this nightly routine almost more than the girls did.

'No, surely you're mistaken. It was my turn last night.'

'No, Maman, last night was *The Frog Prince*. It's your turn tonight.'

'And what story would you like to hear?'

'My favourite one, silly.'

Roman growled softly, and Tatiana looked apologetic enough for long enough, before reaching out a hand towards Ella to pull her on to the bed. Dorcas stalked over to her doggy bed in the corner of the room, seemingly content that she had successfully herded her entire family into one room.

As she sat down on the edge of the bed, next to her husband and children, Ella felt wrapped in a cocoon of unconditional love. Her family, all joyous, beautiful, beaming, happy and safe.

'Once upon a time, there was a sweet little maiden and whoever laid eyes upon her couldn't help but love her, nor help but remark on the beautiful red velvet cape her grandmother had given her...'

She looked at her husband and he didn't need to hear the words that cried through her heart straight to his. For Ella did believe in fairy tales now that they'd both found their happy-ever-after.

* * * * *

Wrapped up in the drama of
Taming the Big Bad Billionaire?
*Enter Pippa Roscoe's passionate world
with these other stories!*

Claimed for the Greek's Child
Reclaimed by the Powerful Sheikh
Virgin Princess's Marriage Debt
Demanding His Billion-Dollar Heir

Available now!

COMING NEXT MONTH FROM

⬢ HARLEQUIN
PRESENTS

Available June 16, 2020

#3825 THE ITALIAN IN NEED OF AN HEIR
Cinderella Brides for Billionaires
by Lynne Graham
No one rejects Raffaele Manzini. Gorgeous, ruthless and successful, he gets what he wants. But strong-willed Maya Campbell is his biggest challenge yet. For if he's to acquire the company he most desires, they must marry and have a child...

#3826 A BABY TO BIND HIS INNOCENT
The Sicilian Marriage Pact
by Michelle Smart
Claudia Buscetta's wedding night with Ciro Trapani is everything she dreamed of—but then she overhears Ciro's confession: the marriage was his way of avenging his father. Claudia prepares to walk away forever...only to discover she's pregnant!

#3827 VOWS TO SAVE HIS CROWN
by Kate Hewitt
Rachel Lewis is completely thrown by Prince Mateo's convenient proposal. She's known him for years, and has secretly yearned for him every single second. It's an irresistible offer...but can she really share his palace—and his royal bed—without getting hurt?

#3828 HIRED BY THE IMPOSSIBLE GREEK
by Clare Connelly
Scientist-turned-schoolteacher Amelia agrees to a summer job in Greece caring for Santos Anastakos's young son. Her priority is the little boy, *not* the outrageous and irresistible billionaire who hired her. Even if their chemistry is, scientifically speaking, off the charts!

HPCNMRA0620

#3829 CLAIMING HIS UNKNOWN SON
Spanish Secret Heirs
by Kim Lawrence

Marisa was the first and last woman Roman Bardales proposed to, and her stark refusal turned his heart to stone. Now he's finally discovered the lasting effects of their encounter: his son! And he's about to stake his claim to his child...

#3830 A FORBIDDEN NIGHT WITH THE HOUSEKEEPER
by Heidi Rice

Maxim Durand can't believe that housekeeper Cara has inherited *his* vineyard. But bartering with the English beauty isn't going to be simple... As their desire explodes into passionate life, the question is: What does Maxim want? His rightful inheritance... or Cara?

#3831 HER WEDDING NIGHT NEGOTIATION
by Chantelle Shaw

Kindhearted Leah Ashbourne's wedding *has* to go ahead to save her mother from ruin. So the collapse of her engagement is a disaster! Until billionaire Marco arrives, needing her help. Leah is ready to negotiate with him—but her price is marriage!

#3832 REVELATIONS OF HIS RUNAWAY BRIDE
by Kali Anthony

From the moment Thea Lambros is forced to walk down the aisle toward Christo Callas, her only thought is escape. But when coolly brilliant Christo interrupts her getaway, Thea meets her electrifying match. Because her new husband unleashes an unexpected fire within her...

Love Harlequin romance?

DISCOVER.

Be the first to find out about promotions, news and exclusive content!

Facebook.com/HarlequinBooks

Twitter.com/HarlequinBooks

Instagram.com/HarlequinBooks

Pinterest.com/HarlequinBooks

ReaderService.com

EXPLORE.

Sign up for the Harlequin e-newsletter and download a free book from any series at **TryHarlequin.com**

CONNECT.

Join our Harlequin community to share your thoughts and connect with other romance readers!
Facebook.com/groups/HarlequinConnection